# What the critics are saying…

*5 Angels!* "This is a can't miss tale of oceanic proportions." ~ *Sarah, Fallen Angel Reviews*

"...a delightfully humorous story with the sort of hero that we all dream of and an extremely engaging heroine." ~ *Mireya, A Romance Review*

# Wet and Wilde

Tawny Taylor

WET AND WILDE
An Ellora's Cave Publication, March 2005

Ellora's Cave Publishing, Inc.
1337 Commerce Drive Suite #13
Stow, Ohio 44224

ISBN #1419951602


Other available formats: ISBN MS Reader (LIT), Adobe (PDF), Rocketbook (RB), Mobipocket (PRC) & HTML



Edited by: *Martha Punches*
Cover art by: *Syneca*

# Warning:

The following material contains graphic sexual content meant for mature readers. *Wet and Wilde* has been rated *E-rotic* by a minimum of three independent reviewers.

Ellora's Cave Publishing offers three levels of Romantica™ reading entertainment: S (S-ensuous), E (E-rotic), and X (X-treme).

S-*ensuous* love scenes are explicit and leave nothing to the imagination.

E-*rotic* love scenes are explicit, leave nothing to the imagination, and are high in volume per the overall word count. In addition, some E-rated titles might contain fantasy material that some readers find objectionable, such as bondage, submission, same sex encounters, forced seductions, etc. E-rated titles are the most graphic titles we carry; it is common, for instance, for an author to use words such as "fucking", "cock", "pussy", etc., within their work of literature.

X-*treme* titles differ from E-rated titles only in plot premise and storyline execution. Unlike E-rated titles, stories designated with the letter X tend to contain controversial subject matter not for the faint of heart.

## Also by Tawny Taylor:

Passion In A Pear Tree

Tempting Fate

Lessons in Lust Major

Private Games

Ellora's Cavemen, Tales from the Temple IV:

Body Chemistry

# Wet and Wilde

# Chapter One
## *Another girl's night – in hell.*

If there was one thing Jane Wilde knew it was that she'd trade her left boob to avoid another pathetic Saturday night at Diana's, swapping complaints about the slim pickin's in the man department. In fact, she'd give up both boobs. Her stiff neck and shoulder muscles would thank her.

She sure didn't want to be reminded of how pitiful her love life was at the moment.

Bucket of popcorn the size of a small bathtub in one hand, a glass of diet cola, since she was on a diet, in the other, she took her prescribed seat on the couch. "Please tell me we aren't watching another vampire flick. I'm vamped out. And if I didn't know better," she paused to stab at her best friend and confidante, Diana, with a finger, "I'd swear your teeth have grown at least a quarter inch."

"Nope. No vamps today." Diana gave Jane a toothy grin and scooped up a handful of popcorn, leaving half of it trailing over Jane's lap. "It's mermaids! *Splash*."

"Oh God, spare me." Jane slid deeper into the super-plush cushions of Diana's sky-blue couch.

"It has Cher in it. How could it be that bad?" Carmen, Jane's other best friend, asked as she rounded the corner from the kitchen, her expression chock-full of wide-eyed hope. "Have you seen it?"

"It's not *that* movie." Jane fought back the urge to roll her eyes skyward. "Although I wouldn't want to see that one, either. This is the movie with that blonde—what's her name?—walking naked around New York. It's older than I am, and even lamer. The only good thing about it is Tom Hanks. Couldn't you find something better?" She dumped half her cola down her throat, about ready to hit the harder stuff. If this night was going to be salvaged, she'd need something with a lot more kick, like tequila. "Why can't we watch a movie that has nothing to do with mythological creatures, whether they live in dungeons or the sea?"

"Because those creatures are mysterious—sexy!" Diana waggled her eyebrows, her eyes the size of silver dollars, and punched her. "Have you ever considered the possibilities?"

"Possibilities?" Jane shook her head, ignoring Diana's jab to her shoulder. "Not since I quit believing in the Easter Bunny."

Diana gave her another nudge. "Scoot over and quit being such a grouch."

Jane shot Diana an intentionally exaggerated look of admonishment and complied, giving her just enough room for her skinny ass to fit between the couch arm and Jane's admittedly wider one. "Next week, I choose."

Diana clucked her tongue and shook her head. "You know the rules, the hostess picks the movie. And next week it's Carmen's turn."

Carmen nodded her head.

This time Jane didn't bother stopping her eyes from rolling. "And Carmen calls you from the video store every time."

"Well, if you answered your phone occasionally," Carmen piped in, sounding a touch defensive, "I'd call you, too."

"You both know why I don't. That man won't stop calling me, divorce or not. He's such a control freak."

"Maybe it's time to change your number," Diana offered.

Jane shot up from the couch. Yep, it was definitely time for that drink. She drained her glass on her way to the kitchen, leaving the other two women to their discussion about next week's torture. No doubt it would be some sort of monster-mermaid-superman flick. If only she had something better to do!

She stooped down, rummaging through Diana's eternally well-stocked refrigerator. The woman kept enough food in there for an army, and ate a truckload at every meal.

Jane hated her…kinda.

"Where're the wine coolers?" she shouted.

"Carmen's polishing off the last one," Diana answered. "You want me to go to the store for more?"

Drag! No alcohol? A movie released before she had filled out her first bra, and nothing to sweeten the deal. Could this night be any worse? "No, that's okay." She refilled her glass with diet cola and headed back to the living room.

Both ladies smiled at her. Smiled like they'd just signed a pact with the devil. Like they'd just enlisted her in the army. Like they'd just promised her life in return for…something.

*Uh oh.* "What?"

"We have an idea," Diana stood and reached for Jane's arm.

"Yeah, a really great idea." Carmen reached for the other arm.

Sandwiched between two conniving women? That was one place she didn't want to be. She tugged but quickly realized they weren't going to let her go. "What kind of idea?" She really didn't want to know.

Carmen giggled. "Since your birthday's coming up—"

"It was last month," Jane interrupted.

"Even better!" Diana released her arm and gave her shoulders a sound shove, knocking her backward onto the couch. "Sit. Shut up. And listen. This is for your own good."

Diana could sure be one bossy bitch! It almost pissed Jane off the way Diana was literally pushing her around. She prepared to deliver a choice word or two, but reminded herself of the past six months.

Yep, after holding Jane up for six months, the least her well-meaning friend had earned was a license to shove.

Jane glanced at Carmen, and Carmen gave her a reassuring smile.

"Okay," she said on a sigh. "What's this great idea?"

"For your birthday, we'd like to give you a wish. A makeover. New clothes, new attitude on life. What do you say?"

"New attitude? What's wrong with the one I have?" She wasn't sure she liked what their grand scheme implied. Was she that pitiable? Were her clothes that outdated?

"Nothing, really." Carmen sat on the coffee table. "But we just thought you could use—" She shrugged. "Something to make you feel better, now that— Well, you know."

Did they have to keep mentioning that? "I'm fine—outside of my phone ringing off the damn hook, and the two people I call my best friends bull-dogging me into something I don't want to do."

Diana sat on the table and shoved Carmen aside. "You're making her feel worse. Let me try." Diana sighed. "Listen, sweetie. Everyone who goes through a change in life—good or bad—has to adjust. That goes for you, too. And to ease that adjustment, it's good to do something positive, for yourself."

"Like get surgery to make myself look like Pamela Anderson?" Jane asked, fighting a smile.

"Sure!" Carmen nodded her head.

"Seriously." Diana gave Jane a swift smack on the thigh—*ouch*! "Get with the program here. Isn't there anything you have wanted to do for yourself? Something that's been nagging at you for a long, long time?"

"I've wanted to get plastic surgery," Carmen interjected. "I'd love to look like Pamela—at least from the neck to about here." She motioned just below her very flat boobs.

Diana smiled. "Okay, sweetie." She gave Carmen's shoulder a squeeze. "We'll get you that surgery when your birthday comes."

Carmen grinned, her pink-tinged face getting even redder, clashing with her carrot-hued hair. "You will! Gosh, that's mighty nice of you!"

Jane watched Carmen, all aglow, and thought about the possibilities. Okay, the idea of having a wish was kind of cool. Something for herself? Something that would make her feel better? Then, the idea struck her. "I've always wanted to learn how to swim."

In an instant, memories of sultry days on the beach with her brothers and sisters came to mind. Days when they enjoyed the fresh coolness of the sea while she sat frozen by fear at the shore, willing herself to take a leap into that terrifying, roiling mass. She couldn't remember exactly when that fear had surfaced, vaguely recalled nearly drowning as a young child. But she sure would like to shake it now.

Diana's smile couldn't get any bigger than it was, and dread slipped down Jane's spine.

"Perfect," Diana said, slapping her hands on her thighs. "I know the perfect person to teach you, too. I mean I don't *know* him personally, but I know of him. He's a world-class swimmer and to-die-for to boot."

"No way." Jane shot to her feet. She was at least twenty pounds overweight, and the Slim Fast shakes weren't doing a bit of good. God, she looked terrible in a swimsuit! Jiggly thighs, an ass that made J-Lo's look tiny…

Diana stopped her before she was completely on her feet and knocked her back on her ass. "You're not backing out. Not a chance. I'm calling. I'm scheduling your class. And I'm taking you, and there isn't a damn thing you can do about it."

*Except not show up.*

"And don't think you can hide from me." Diana finished, as if she could read Jane's mind. "I will find you, and you will go. If it makes you feel any better, I'll take the class with you."

"Great. So, when I drown, I can take you down with me." Jane crossed her arms over her chest. Granted, Diana had been a lifesaver—literally—recently, but that didn't give her the right to force her to do anything. Last time Jane checked she was over eighteen—by a few years.

Besides, the idea of standing mostly unclothed next to emaciated Diana was enough to make her vomit.

"It'll be worth it," Diana said, shoveling a mouthful of popcorn into her mouth. She chewed and swallowed then washed it down with a swig of her calorie-laden Kahlua concoction. "We'll celebrate by going on a cruise. Anywhere in the world you want to go. My treat."

"Did I miss something? Did you get a promotion?" Since when did Diana have that kind of money to burn? A cruise? Wow, Jane had watched commercials, read catalogues, dreamed of going on a ship ever since she'd religiously watched Love Boat as a kid. "Anywhere in the world?"

She'd always wondered if the Caribbean was really as beautiful as the pictures. She'd booked a cruise for herself, once. When she'd frozen at the dock, stopped cold in terror, and refused to go on board, the ship went out to sea without her.

Diana shrugged her shoulders in dismissal. "I guess we'll just have to go without you, then."

*Go without me!* That day had left one lasting impression. She'd never be left behind again.

"Okay. I'll do it."

Her reluctant acquiescence was greeting by a loud round of whoops and hollers, and more than a few high-fives.

When the roar died down, four words struck her mind and turned her stomach, "Great!" Diana announced with a flourish. "I knew you'd say that. Classes start tomorrow."

# Chapter Two

*Interesting things happen at the bottom of swimming pools.*

"Where is the rest of your bathing suit?" Jane stared gape-mouthed at Diana. Three triangular patches covered her tits and pussy.

"What?" Diana spun around.

Okay—there were four, one that didn't come close to covering her ass. "That thing is obscene! This is a family center, you know. You can't go out there looking like that."

"This is fine. You need to loosen up." Diana tugged on Jane's shoulder strap. "You're wearing too much material. That thing'll drag you to the bottom of the pool for sure. You might as well be wearing a ball gown."

"Well, at least no one will see what I haven't trimmed today."

Diana slammed her locker shut. "I'm shaved clean as a baby's ass. No problem there."

*She is? I thought only porn stars and strippers did that.* "I don't care." She shoved an oversized t-shirt at her friend. "Wear this or I won't leave this locker room."

"Okay." Diana slid it over her head and poked her arms through the holes. "Whatever it takes to get you in the water." She tossed her head, sending her gold hair cascading down her back and shoulders.

Yep, Jane hated Diana...sorta.

They padded through the shower room toward the glass door at the end, Jane's flip flops striking the tile floor with an obnoxious *slap-slap* sound. Maybe she could have skipped them, but she'd read about the dangers of fungus. This place had to be a breeding ground.

Diana pushed the door open, and Jane scanned the crowd before stepping foot in the huge room.

The first thing she saw, lots of little kids, some in the pool suspended by orange balloons on their arms. *Did those come in adult size?* They looked pretty handy.

Other kids were kicking their way across the deep end of the pool—my God, their parents put them in twelve feet of water!—with the aid of a white foam board. A couple of young women stood on the side of the pool, whistles caught between their teeth, arms crossed over red t-shirted chests. The whistles sounded, the ear-splitting whirr ricocheting off the concrete walls and high ceiling. "Time's up. Out of the pool." The kids, who all made it to the opposite end of the pool, thank God, discarded the foam boards and hauled themselves out of the water.

"Our class starts in a few minutes." Diana stood by Jane's side, leaning casually against the wall.

"Gee, I can hardly—" Jane's breath caught in her throat, trapping the rest of the sentence with it.

Who the hell was that? Staring at her? Blond, tall, built like a god. Holy shit! Her gaze slid lower, taking the bumpy road over bulging chest muscles and a rippling stomach…and lower to a very defined lump housed in thin spandex. No human being deserved to look so…*Damn!*…to be hung like that.

"What's wrong?" Diana asked. "Oh."

Someone slugged Jane's arm, but she didn't care. She let her gaze travel down smooth skin housing bunched quads. Dark, and devoid of hair, his skin looked like it belonged to a water creature.

She could spend all night oiling that body.

She forced her gaze past that glorious sight between his legs—what a crime!—and continued back to his face. His gaze was volcano-hot, dark and penetrating, and riveted to her. Her oxygen-deprived brain screamed at her to take a breath.

She gasped.

He took two long strides toward her, and before she'd filled her lungs completely, he stopped inches away. Staring down from impossible heights, through eyes fringed with lashes of impossible length, and giving her a smile formed by two impossibly perfect lips, he said, "Hi."

She tried to speak. There was no air.

Someone smacked her in the back, and her brain switched back on.

Her lungs filled. "Hi."

"Josh, this is my friend, Jane Wilde."

His eyes flashed as Diana said her name. "Wilde, eh?"

She felt a blush spread over her face. "I'm not, really, but I could be. Er, I could try—" Shit! Had that just come out of her mouth? "I meant to say—"

"Not Jane Wilde?" he asked, that smile still in place. Perfect white teeth flashed bright against his suntanned skin.

"No…I mean, I'm not really wild."

She'd thought it impossible, but that gaze of his just got hotter. She was sure she'd burn up if she didn't glance away.

"For some reason, I don't believe that." His voice was so low and smooth it seemed to vibrate inside her body. A crazy charge shot down her spine and settled between her legs. Her pussy was wet. Just like that.

"Don't believe a word she says," Diana half-spoke, half-laughed. "Well, are we ready to jump in the pool?"

"I am." *Anything to cool off. I'm going to combust.* Jane was burning from the inside out. Her blood was literally boiling. Her muscles tingled. Her crotch thrummed. Her tits stood at attention. What man did that to a woman with just a look?

She walked to the side of the pool and glanced down.

The heat evaporated from her body, and she shivered. That was a lot of water!

"Diana told me you're phobic." His voice caressed her jittery nerves, instantly calming them. How the hell did he do that?

She turned around. Bad move. He had one hell of a fuck-me look! It took every ounce of her strength to remain composed. There were children about. If she were alone with him, she just might throw him down and make him pay for that sexy stare…

Her pussy clenched. Hot juices puddled in her bathing suit bottom.

He licked his lips, and she felt the sudden urge to do the same. She tasted something. Salty, musky. He smiled.

She was losing her mind! Fingertips materialized out of thin air, tiptoeing over her body, up her spine, down her arms, down her neck.

*What the hell?* No one was touching her.

*Oh, yeah...* The unseen fingers teased her nipples through her bathing suit, making small circles and then tugging them to aching erection. Others skittered down her stomach and over her mound.

*Mmmm. If only they'd move a little lower.* They did, and her knees turned to marshmallow.

She sat; her feet dropped into the pool.

*Ahhh...*

"Look at that! She's got her feet in the water. That's more than I've ever seen her do outside of a bath tub." Diana sat beside her. "How're you doing?"

Still confused by the strange and wonderful sensations humming through her body, she simply nodded.

"I'm so proud of you for doing this." Diana gave her shoulders a squeeze.

She looked up from the cold blue water. There were other people all around. Where had they come from?

"Okay. Time to get started." The god—what was his name? Joe? No, Josh. Yes! Josh—gripped his whistle in his fist. "Everyone in the pool. I need you lined up on this side." His leg brushed her shoulder—satiny smooth. She leaned against it. "You, too, Jane."

His voice hummed in her head and between her legs. Her pussy throbbed. She slid into the water, thankful for the chill on her skin.

"Look at you! You're doing it." Diana slipped into the water beside her, giving her an encouraging smile. Then her brows drew together and her eyes squinted. "Have you been lying all this time?"

"No. I'm scared to death of water."

"Well, you're neck-deep in it."

Her eyes dropped, skimming over the surface. "Oh God!" She felt the first blade of panic pierce her brain. Her legs stiffened.

"Jane," Mr. Perfect said. "Look at me."

She looked. Hell, she couldn't *not* look.

There was that mind-melting gaze again. Dark and deep. She felt like it was digging through her brain, rummaging through her secrets. Her body tingled all over. Her limbs came alive. He handed down a white foam board. "Hold this in front of you and swim across the pool."

A gift? For her? His first gift. She sighed, hugged it to her chest, and smiled.

He laughed, and she snapped out of her daze. Her face this close to bursting into flames, she turned from him. And holding the foam board in her hands, she let her body float for a moment, absorbing the chill into her core. It was a strange feeling, hot and cold. She kicked her legs.

That felt different, too. The water slithered around her ankles as her feet moved. She kicked harder, and the water moved across her stomach and chest and along her sides.

Before she knew it, the opposite pool side was in front of her. She gripped it, bewildered. Had she just swum across the pool?

Diana floated at her side. "My God! You did it! I'm so happy for you!" Her face was alight with a bright grin.

Pride and surprise shot through Jane's body. "I didn't even realize what I was doing."

"See? It isn't so bad, is it?"

She glanced at the man who'd somehow talked her into swimming without saying more than a handful of words. He smiled at her.

Her heart did a little jig. She had the overwhelming urge to return to him. She had to be near him. She gripped that foam board in her hands and pushed her feet against the slick pool tiles, propelling herself forward. Her gaze remained on his face as she kicked her way back across the pool.

"Very good, Jane." His voice thrummed through her body as she stopped before him. "You're a natural. You've taken to water like a regular mermaid."

She felt a silly grin spread over her face. "Well, I never expected it to be so easy."

"Neither did I," Diana said from behind her. "My God, she wouldn't get near a birdbath before today."

Jane didn't appreciate that stab, especially when it was said in front of Mr. Tall, Dark and Sexy, and set out to prove just how brave and able she was. She tossed the board aside in favor of a smaller pool noodle, turned back around and took several more laps across the pool just to show her. She was no chicken! *Birdbath, my ass!*

"Jane, you must get out of the water now." His voice hit the pit of her stomach.

"Just a minute more." She flung her arms over the noodle and kicked away from the poolside. But, when she was almost halfway across the pool, someone bumped her, knocking the noodle out from under her chest, and she slipped below the surface. She thrashed, seeing white everywhere. Noise exploded in her ears, magnified to deafening volume by the water.

She gave up and drifted lower. Her lungs screamed for air, and she swallowed against the urge to inhale. Her feet hit the scratchy concrete bottom, and she pushed up, her arms reaching toward the silver, shimmering surface above. No sooner did she break through it then she was back on the bottom again.

Suddenly, he was there, and every nerve ending charged to life. He looked her in the eye. "You're okay. Don't panic."

Had he just spoken to her? How? *Get me the hell outta here before I die. This is no time for hallucinations.*

He chuckled in her head.

How the hell did someone do that? The sounds vibrated through her whole body, to her toes and eyelashes. Her stomach and fingertips. A warm throb settled between her legs.

She was getting horny? At the bottom of a pool? What the heck was that all about?

# Chapter Three

*Without the chase, the prize would be as meaningful as mud.*

This was the one. She would be a perfect mate. His gaze settled on her face as he calmed her and enumerated her attributes. She had beautiful, classic features that would set the goddesses afire with jealousy. Impossibly long eyelashes fringed eyes the color of milk chocolate. Her nose was pert but slender, raised at the tip to give her just enough sass to amuse him. Her lips…those lips. He already knew they tasted of the sweetest nectar in paradise. How he wished to kiss them now!

Yet, he resisted. This woman—this human—possessed a fiery will, and would need some coaxing before she would fully submit to him.

He would settle for nothing less than full submission—of body, mind and spirit.

Besides, there was much to appreciate in the chase.

He mentally murmured more soothing words to her, taking full advantage of his powers over humans. Thankfully, she calmed, allowing him a brief but welcome opportunity to see her as she might be in his world—not that he'd ever expect her to follow him there.

Selkies had mated with humans for ages, but the hazards of falling in love with one were well known. It was much safer this way—to mate and leave. The land dwellers would raise his child until he was old enough to join his father in their world below.

But, as he watched her chestnut hair drift around her face and over her shoulders, flirting with breasts so ripe and firm they beckoned his touch, he found himself wondering if it might be possible…

Her panic sliced through him, cutting that thought off before he'd finished it.

Perhaps not.

Testing her powers of intuition, wanting to sense whether she felt the connection between them, he reached out, touching her between those luscious breasts. Her heartbeat, jackrabbit quick, increased in response to his touch.

Yes, very good. Her body was willing, even if her mind was not yet ready. His own reacted in a primal response, blood pumping through his body in hot waves, pooling between his legs until his erection pushed against the containment of his swim trunks.

*Hush, love. You're safe. Can you see how magical this place is below the surface? You came from water. It's a part of you.* He palmed her cheek before letting his hand slide lower to grasp her neck. Her hair twined around his fingers, dancing upon the shifting currents like tiny fish.

*Get me the hell outta here. I'm no more water than you are frickin' gold! And how the hell are we talking?*

He let his fingertips stray lower and to the left, tracing the line of her collarbone before dipping between her tits and skirting the fullness of a breast. Then it continued down, following the line of her torso. Damn, she was perfect! Her body was soft, as a woman's should be. Her skin was smooth under his touch, velvety. Her energy, and the unique taste of her filled the water surrounding them, sending his nerves aflame. His groin ached, his cock throbbed, and only one image played through his mind—bending her over and fucking her until he dropped dead away.

*And unless you're going to rescue me, get your fuckin' hands off! I'm dying down here!*

He couldn't help smiling. Yes, a fiery sprite, she was, one that would make Coventina, the goddess he most adored—for her spunk, of course—hang her head in shame.

*As long as we're together, you won't die.*

*Nice, buddy. What kind of nut job are you?* Using her feet, she pushed up from the concrete floor, scooping water into her cupped hands as she swam to the surface.

He followed her and the sounds, sights and smells of the world outside the water assaulted him as he broke the surface. Wrapping one protective arm around Jane's narrow waist, he gave her time to catch her breath. She sputtered and sagged against him in relief.

Her soft body against his made every muscle tense. His cock shot to full erection, his internal engine switched to high gear as his heart pumped blood through every miniscule part of him. His heart's quickened thump pounded in his ear, revved even more as he cupped her ass with his free hand and held her tight against him. His legs kicked slowly, keeping them both afloat.

Damn, how he wished they were in murky waters! The toxic chemicals in the pool water left it as clear as the calmest sea, and offered no opportunity for further exploration of the body pressed firmly against him.

And what exploration he would like to have, particularly of the delicious juncture between her thighs. He licked his lips as he mentally tasted her.

Sweet, mellow.

"Are you going to take me to the side, or are you just going to stay here in the middle of the pool and cop a feel?"

He laughed. Her sharp wit delighted him. "I don't see you objecting."

"Like hell, I'm not!" She shoved at his chest, but he held her fast, purposefully molding her body to his and appreciating every place their skin touched.

"Truly, you don't wish me to release you, do you?" His skin was ablaze as nerve endings erupted like tiny volcanoes, sending molten lava through his veins. His cock reared up, ready to delve into her juices, plunder her into the submission he knew she yearned for. And yet, he knew he could do nothing but deliver her to the side of the pool and release her.

His heart sank at the thought. Now that he had found her, he didn't want to let her go.

Still in the middle of the swimming pool, he let his grip slacken.

She, of her own will, wrapped her legs and arms around him, pressing into him. "No. Not here! Don't let me go out here. I'll drown."

"Look at me." He forced his voice into a command when he would have rather sung. Nothing felt better than a woman pressed tightly against him. Not the pressure of the heavy seas upon his shoulders, or the joy of a swim with dolphins.

She obeyed.

Yes, she would do nicely. Her will was strong, but not impossible to bend. Like a willow. Her gaze met his and her eyes widened.

"You're always safe with me. I will never let any harm come to you."

"But—"

"I'll protect you, always. I promise."

Her lovely mouth, still glistening with moisture, quivered, and he yearned to kiss away the movement. His entire body took in her essence, her sweet smell, her taste, her softness against his hardness. It was pure murder to hold back, to resist his increasingly urgent need to mate—in the middle of that pool. In the midst of children's laughter and splashing earth dwellers careening through the silky waters.

The gods were punishing him!

His cock throbbed with a need so great he had no choice. He moved quick, delivering her to the tile-coated side of the pool, and in one swift motion he set her above him. She looked down with such confusion on her face he had to smile, despite the ache between his legs, through his gut…in his heart.

"Thanks, I think," she stammered. She didn't move, didn't turn away.

He let his gaze visibly linger on her smooth legs then travel slowly up to the dark gap between them. She remained still, seemingly open to his visual investigation. He checked her face for a reaction and wasn't disappointed.

It was a pleasant, cock-heating shade of pink.

He licked his lips, which had gone dry, despite the fact that he was still submerged chest-deep in water. "Will I see you next week?"

"I…er, I'm not sure."

"I would be very disappointed if you didn't come."

"I will then. I'd hate to see you disappointed." She stood and took a single step backward, the slight increase in distance stretching the invisible connection between them. The energy dancing between them faded to a dull glow, which he knew only he could see.

"Good, and wear a different bathing suit, one with less material. It'll be better for swimming." He sent her a deliberately heated glance.

She smiled. What a glorious sight! "That was about the worst line I've ever heard." She scooped up her plastic shoes and towel and wrapped the white terrycloth around her waist. "It was good meeting you."

"You, too, Jane Wilde." He let her name echo through his head as he watched her walk away, admiring the sway of her hips, the roundness of her ass pushing the snowy material out from her backside.

She would be a delight to bed—passionate, submissive, eager to please, yet a firebrand that would test him in every way.

He must mate with her. As soon as possible.

His cock reared once more.

* * * * *

Jane shook away the sound of his voice, still echoing through her head as she walked through the locker room. Her body tingled, from hair roots to toes, almost as if she'd just climaxed. Hell, if she didn't know better, she'd swear she had.

Diana was fully dressed, sitting on a wood bench, her hair dry, make-up in place.

Jane dropped on the bench next to Diana, her legs wobbly as jelly and her heart still thumping in her ears. Her pussy was on fire, tingly and wet, the muscles twitching like they did after an orgasm. "Where the hell were you? Doing your hair while I nearly drowned?"

"Nearly drowned?" Diana screwed her picture-perfect features into a mask of disbelief. "You did not! Before you even lost that pool noodle, that gorgeous swimming instructor dove in after you. You're so melodramatic."

"Well, I was under water long enough for you to dress, apply your make-up, and do your hair. That has to tell you something."

"It tells me you were in the pool catching a feel—not that I'd blame you." Diana gave her an elbow jab in the ribs. "What did I tell you? To die for, isn't he?"

"If he's so great, why aren't you going for him?" Jane stood and rubbed her ribcage. That jab smarted. Little bitch! Just another sensation to add to the myriad her mind still hadn't sorted through yet—warmth in places she hadn't felt come alive in ages, tingling, throbbing, aching, and lots of confusion in the brain. She opened her locker and pulled out her clothes, waiting patiently for Diana's smartass comeback.

"I tried. I'm not his type."

Well, now, that was a stunner! Diana was every man's type...or so Jane had always assumed. Gorgeous, with a perfect body, legs that went forever, a waist at least a handful of inches smaller than her own, and round, perky tits...what wouldn't the guy like? "Really? Why am I having a hard time believing that?"

Diana nodded. "I think he figures I'm too high maintenance, which I am."

Jane pulled the towel off her still electrified body and rubbed her hair dry, licking the salty taste from her lips. Salt? Where had that come from? "Smart man. I like him already." She went to a private stall to change. She never had been comfortable undressing in front of anyone, even Diana.

When she returned to the main area, Diana was leaning against the locker, backpack slung over one shoulder, purse over the other. "Seriously, I can't believe what you did in that pool. That was amazing. You're coming back next week, aren't you?"

"I don't know. I told him I would."

"That's great! You did way better than I ever expected." She gave Jane a solid thump on the back. "You're a real trooper, made outta tougher stuff than I thought. I'm proud of you."

"Yeah, yeah. It's not like I went deep sea diving or anything. It was a half hour in a swimming pool." She left the building, wondering exactly what the hell had happened in there.

Not only had she seemingly conquered the worst of her fear of water, but she'd also experienced one of the most erotic moments in her life...twelve feet under the surface! Not that she was about to tell Diana that. After all, even the though of it—which still sent ripples of pleasure through her entire body—was outrageous. How could she possibly explain it?

# Chapter Four

*The mind plays the most fascinating tricks on itself sometimes.*

"It's early." Diana eyed Jane from the passenger seat before returning her attention to the vanity mirror glued to the back of the car's sun visor. "Want to get something to eat? Swimming makes me hungry."

"Everything makes you hungry. I'll bet eating makes you hungry." Jane started the car. She still hadn't fully recovered from whatever had happened in that pool, if anything had actually happened. As time passed, and the twitching between her legs eased, she was convinced it had been in her imagination. Some kind of psycho mechanism to protect her from the horror of nearly drowning.

Who knew psycho mechanisms could be so damn…exhilarating?

One thing was for certain, that gorgeous hunk of man had been all too real. From the tip of his head to the soles of his feet, living breathing, hunky heaven.

A bit of a mystery, too. There was something…what was it? Something dark and mysterious about him. Something that made him different from every man she'd ever met. She couldn't put his face from her mind, or the sound of his frolicking voice from echoing through her body. It kind of vibrated through her, like a current of low voltage electricity.

Unforgettable. She'd have some dandy dreams tonight, she had no doubt. Maybe a few pre-sleep fantasies while she was at it. There was one other fact she couldn't doubt, his cock had been large and ready. A blade of heat shot to her pussy, making it instantly slick.

Wow! She couldn't remember the last time a simple thought had made her horny. This was something! Maybe she'd get more for her supposed birthday makeover-slash-wish her friends had promised than she'd bargained for.

About twelve inches more, if her eyes hadn't been deceiving her—God forbid! She'd never had anything bigger than average, whatever that was. It wasn't like she'd bothered to measure. What did it feel like to fuck twelve inches of cock? Her pussy began to weep in response to that unspoken question.

"Hello! Earth to Jane!" Diana waved her hands in front of Jane's nose. "You still with me?"

"Yeah. Where'd you think I'd gone?"

"Somewhere far away. And gauging from the very strange look on your face, filled with lots of yummy man-meat." She snorted, obviously amused with herself.

"Where are we going?" Jane refused to encourage Diana. If she did, the conversation would get slimy in a hurry. "I just want to get home."

"What's the big hurry? Don't tell me you've been holdin' out on me! Do you have a sex slave locked in the basement?"

"God, no!" Even without help, the conversation had taken a nosedive. "Where do you get this stuff from?"

Looking quite coy and pleased, Diana simply shrugged her shoulders. "A girl can dream, can't she?"

"You? What do you have to dream about? You can have any man you want. Now, where are we going?"

Diana didn't speak.

Clearly Diana didn't care to answer the first question, nor did she seem to care where they went to eat. Without asking a third time, Jane shifted the car into drive and headed down the street, turning into the nearest restaurant's parking lot.

"Where are you going?"

"You didn't tell me you had someplace special in mind." Jane put the car into park. *What's up with Diana today*? If Jane didn't know better, she'd swear Diana had been the one to nearly drown, lose a few thousand brain cells.

"Yes! I mean, no." Diana shook her head. "But, I'm in the mood for some Italian. Let's hit Giovanni's up the street."

"What are you up to?" She eyed her friend, taking care to note shifting eyes mostly hidden by black-framed shades.

"Nothing."

"Bullshit." Blinking against the early evening sun hanging low over the horizon, Jane dug in her purse for her sunglasses.

"I'm hungry. Is it a crime to crave Italian food?"

Maybe she was being a little overly suspicious. "Okay. Italian it is," she half-breathed, half-spoke. She drove down the street in the opposite direction, parked the car in the lot, and half-expecting a group of friends to jump out and yell surprise, Jane walked into the restaurant's quiet, cozy interior.

No rounds of clichéd songs.

No surprises whatsoever.

Whew! A relief.

"Well, look who's here!" Diana caught her by the elbow and dragged her past the hostess wearing a dazed expression and a black mini-dress that hugged her curves like a race car.

What was Diana dragging her into now?

"Hi there." It was that voice. His voice.

Jane dug her heels into the carpet. Her heart came to a dead stop. Her face heated. Her pussy clenched as juices drenched her panties.

Diana jerked on her arm. "Is that any way to act?" she whispered in Jane's ear. "The man is speaking to you."

"I'm trying!" She pulled her arm free from Diana's vice grip and forced herself to look at him.

Oh wow! She hadn't thought her panties could get any wetter. She was wrong.

He looked amazing. His snug black shirt caressed every angle and plane of his chest and stomach. The ones she'd been pressed up against such a short time ago… Oh shit! She might just come right there.

She needed to sit. And she needed something to drink. Something cold. Her throat was so dry she feared she'd choke on words. "Hi."

She managed that much. That had to count for something.

"Please," he motioned to the bench seat next to him, "have a seat. I was just about ready to order. Would you ladies like something special?"

She sat and scooted into the corner of the L-shaped booth. Josh sat next to her, sliding much too close for her comfort—okay, maybe not quite close enough. Diana pinned her in by coming around to the other side. Sandwiched between a hot guy who made her brain melt, and a friend who suddenly felt like a third wheel…or a lifeline, Jane wasn't sure which it was.

At this point, she wasn't sure of anything, outside of the way her body was heating from the inside out, her pussy was dripping, her tits were aching, and her mind was racing to places and thoughts she'd never visited before.

The man hadn't done anything but invite her to sit! Good God, what would she do if he actually touched her!

"Can I order you something to drink?" His voice hummed through her body, sending another wave of warmth to her pussy.

"Ice water?"

"That's it? Wouldn't you like something stronger? Perhaps something rich and creamy?"

What was the man trying to do? Add inches to her hips? "I could take a diet cola…and the ice water." She turned to look at him as he gave the order to the waiter, along with a request for appetizers.

The floor fell away, and it seemed like they were the only people who existed in the world.

Could she breathe? Would her lungs please inflate? Her heart please beat? Her pussy stop dripping? He licked his lips and she mirrored him, tasting salt again. He ran his hand through his hair and she swore she felt the silky softness on her own fingertips. He inhaled deeply and she swore she smelled the musky odor of sex.

Was he wearing some sort of pheromone?

Her mind wasn't her own. Her senses weren't hers, either. It was as though he'd taken over her body. It was a strange yet fascinating feeling.

He smiled. "It's a pleasant surprise, your being here."

"Yeah. I... Hey, wait a minute!" The bizarre sensations halted. Her mind cleared. The rest of the diners dropped right back into their places in the restaurant. One particular inhabitant of the room landed a bit louder than the others. Jane turned to Diana. "You knew, didn't you?"

Diana shook her head. "Knew what?"

"You knew he was here. That's why you made me turn around and come here. Of all places. You never eat Italian food. You say it gives you gas."

Diana's face turned three shades of red. "I've never said any such thing. You're being silly. How could I know he'd be here? I mean, you two were in the pool, and then we left. I didn't have the chance to talk to him."

Okay. Her explanation did make sense, although this situation reeked of conspiracy. "If I find out you did this somehow, I'll bust your ass."

Diana visibly swallowed. She was as guilty as Cain!

"Please, let's forget about that." He lifted a beefy arm, biceps flexing, shoulder muscles bunching. It was a glorious sight. She stared. Her mouth went dry. "Let's have a nice dinner together."

The waiter set several plates of appetizers and her ice water on the table, which she downed it in a chain of desperate gulps. Still, even with that icy liquid cooling her throat and belly, she felt like she was burning up.

Next, she reached for her cola. That she couldn't drink as quickly, but she did swallow half of it before she could stop herself. Sheesh! She'd never been so thirsty before.

"Are you all right?" Diana asked, setting her usual Kahlua concoction down after taking a sip and licking away the creamy white foam from her bottom lip.

"I'm fine." Jane shifted, trying like hell to ease the pulsing between her legs.

Something strong squeezed her shoulder and she dropped her gaze.

His hand. Her shoulder. Here we go!

A blade of warmth shot from her shoulder to her neck, then with her next breath it was right between her legs. The muscles inside clamped closed. She felt herself lean, thanks to just the slightest pressure from that hand on her shoulder.

Her side pressed into his chest. Oh, that was nice! He was warm, snuggly. She could cuddle right in there and stay forever. She felt his breath stirring her hair. His fingers kneaded her shoulder muscles before tiptoeing up her neck. She was lost in the wonderful, mind-blowing sensations of his touch, smell, and feel when Diana's cell phone jangled out Beethoven's Fifth.

Diana punched the call button, said a couple of hushed words and ended the call. She dropped her phone into her purse. "Gotta go."

"Where? What's that all about?"

"I'll tell you later." She stepped away from the table. "Call me when you get home, okay?"

"Sure." Jane's eyelids drooped. She tried to meet Diana's gaze but couldn't quite make it up there. "I'll call you."

Only after Diana was out of sight did Jane remember she'd driven Diana to the restaurant. What was Diana up to? How did she leave?

"Did you pay someone to call Diana away?" She looked at his face, and watched his expression for signs of guilt.

His lips curled up slightly at the corners. *Bingo*! "Maybe. Would it be so bad for me to admit I wanted some time alone with you?"

*No! Would it be so bad to admit I want to fuck your brains out?* She opened her mouth to speak, but didn't get a peep out.

"Mmmm. Love, I like the way you think." He practically purred the words. He reached forward, ran his forefinger down the side of her neck and between her breasts until her shirt's v-neck put a stop to it.

Stupid shirt!

She sucked in a deep breath as her heart started pounding in her ears. What had they been talking about?

"Oyster?" He lifted a shell to her mouth.

"No, thanks. I'm not much for seafood." It didn't even smell appetizing. Ugh! Fishy. She glanced down. Slimy! Nasty!

"You should try it." He transferred the offending item to his own lips. With a toss of his head, the contents of the shell slid into his mouth. Then, with a wicked gleam in his eye, he leaned closer. "Taste."

Jane held her breath, knowing what was coming. The first touch of his lips to hers made her twitch with surprise. His mouth was warm, his lips smooth and soft, moving slowly over hers. Her insides heated, her face heated, her pussy heated.

Damn, what a kiss!

His tongue teased the seam of her lips and she opened to him. He tasted salty and rich. Very yummy, indeed.

He pulled away, and licked his lips. "You like?"

"Mmmm..." She couldn't think, couldn't speak. What this man did to her!

"Would you like another taste?"

"Oh, yeah." She felt so alive! As if every sense was on highest alert. Her ears caught even his faintest breath; her nose, his unique, very masculine scent, even on her own clothes and hands; her eyes, every subtle shift in those amazing features of his; and her skin, his every touch, no matter how soft or innocent.

In the end, those energized, hypersensitive senses were leaving her a horny, quivering, muddy-headed mess.

She watched him eat a second oyster, her gaze glued to his lips. They were slick with butter, looking so tasty, so tempting, she was sure she'd throw him down right there and kiss the living hell out of him.

The waiter stepped up and set their plates before them.

Had she ordered? She didn't recall placing an order. She looked down at her plate. It contained a creamy pasta dish, with seafood. Ugh! She knew she wouldn't have ordered that!

"Is there something wrong?" the waiter asked.

She looked at Josh, and the words sitting at the tip of her tongue refused to spring from her mouth. Instead, she muttered, "Nope. Everything's fine."

The waiter nodded and left.

"You don't like?" Josh whispered, so damn close to her ear, his breath tickled it.

"Like I said, I'm not crazy about seafood. Never have been."

"I'm sorry. I took the liberty of ordering, thinking it would prove what a perfect gentleman I was. I should have asked first."

"No." She looked down. The pasta looked safe. She could easily push the chunks of that white fishy stuff to the side. "It's fine. Thanks." She scooped up a pile of noodles onto her fork.

"Please, allow me." His hand closed around hers, and she swore a bolt of electricity shot up her arm. It stopped her heart for a split second and left every bit of her five foot six inch frame tingly.

*What the hell was that?* She dropped the fork.

He took it up, filled it with noodles and a hunk of the stuff she didn't like and held it before her mouth. "I think there are fewer things sexier than feeding my lover."

"Your lover? Aren't you taking a lot for granted?"

He smiled. What a gorgeous smile! Wow! She had to admit she'd never gotten this close to such a hunk before. Hell, she'd never dreamed about a guy this good looking! There wasn't a single imperfection she could see. Except for maybe an inflated ego, if he really believed she would be his lover after sharing what? A grope in the pool and half a meal.

"I think I'm being very realistic here. Perhaps you're just not ready to accept what's crystal clear to everyone else."

She lifted her hand to her mouth. "Am I drooling or something? I mean, what am I doing that's so obvious?"

"You're dilating."

"What? Dilating?" She wasn't giving birth. What the hell was he talking about?

He chuckled, and the sound bubbled through her body. "Your pupils. They're dilated. And your skin is flushed."

She lifted a hand to her heated cheek in reflex. "Well, maybe I'm a little warm. You have to admit this place is stuffy."

Shaking his head, he directed his gaze lower. "Your nipples are hard."

How could he see that? She was wearing a loose top. It didn't normally emphasize... She glanced down, just to see.

*Shit!*

"Well." She couldn't think of a logical explanation for that one. It wasn't cold in the restaurant.

"Ready to give up yet? Or do you want to hear more?" When she didn't answer, he added, "I have a very acute sense of smell."

"What is that supposed to mean? Do I stink?" She leaned away from him, just in case.

"No." He pressed his chest against her side and whispered in her ear. "You're wet. For me."

Holy shit! He could smell it? Her crotch got that much wetter. Her panties were sopping wet. She bet she could ring them out.

He felt so good pressed against her like that. Hard. Masculine. Sexy. She longed for him to touch her. To explore between her legs. To fuck her.

"Shall we leave?"

She looked down at her full plate. "We should eat, don't you think?"

"Very well. You'll need your strength for later, I suppose." He pulled away from her, only slightly, but enough for her to be keenly, achingly aware of the distance.

It almost hurt.

She tried to concentrate on eating, but it was nearly impossible. Josh seemed to be doing his best to make her feel comfortable, making small talk, asking about her job and friends. Toward the end of the meal, as they sipped their after dinner cocktails, he asked about a more sensitive subject, her love life. Specifically, if she'd ever been in a serious relationship before.

Wasn't the girl supposed to ask questions like that?

"I was married." Had she just admitted that?

"Really?" He lifted those thick eyebrows high, but he didn't ask for more. That was a relief.

"Yeah." She really didn't owe him any more information. After all, he was virtually a stranger—granted a stranger she wished to know better. Still, why did she feel so damn compelled to tell him more?

Must be the oysters. Maybe she was having an allergic reaction!

She pushed her plate away, surprised by how much she'd managed to eat, considering how jittery she was. "The divorce was final a couple of weeks ago."

"I'm sorry." He motioned to the waiter and asked for the check.

"What about you? Have you ever been married?"

"Nope. I haven't thought about it much. Till now."

She fought a chuckle. "You're smooth."

He gifted her with one of those heart-stopping smiles. "You have no idea."

She concentrated on breathing. In…out… How was it he could make her vitals stop with a mere look? And how was it he could make her pussy throb with just a word?

The man was amazing. In every way. Dripping sex appeal from every pore, yet still personable, polite, friendly. He hadn't spoken a single demeaning word to anyone, not even about the waiter—who was less than the best she'd ever had.

Too good to be true. The man was too good to be true. "So, tell me, what is it with you? You're too perfect. What's wrong with you?"

"Me? Perfect? What a nice compliment." He produced a wallet from somewhere and slipped a credit card into the little leather thingy to pay the check with. Reaching over to rub her shoulder with one hand, he handed the waiter the check with the other. "I think you're perfect, too."

"No, seriously." She shifted, so she could be far enough away from him to form a coherent thought. "I wasn't fishing for a compliment. There must be something wrong with you."

"Hmmm…" He lifted his eyes to the ceiling. "Let me think. Well, I can't dance worth a damn. And my friends tell me I eat too much."

Her gaze dropped to the flat plane that was his stomach. The image of that incredible set of abs wet and glistening as she'd seen them earlier flashed through her mind. "Doesn't look like you're hurting there."

"I'm sure it'll catch up to me someday." "Shall we go?" he asked as he accepted his credit card from the waiter and signed the slip. He stood and offered a hand down to her.

She accepted his hand, and damn if that electric current didn't zip up her arm again. Her panties were so damn wet that she could barely walk. Her knees were wobbly. She wrapped her arm around his to steady herself.

Nice! It was nice walking at his side like this. She felt strong yet protected, all at the same time.

He walked her outside, and only then did she realize how late had gotten. The crickets chirred, one of Jane's all time favorite sounds. The parking lot was dark and nearly empty. They stopped at her car, and she rummaged through her purse for her keys. They'd better be there! She wouldn't put it past Diana to steal them so she'd have to accept a ride from Josh.

Then again, a ride from Josh—or on him—might be fun. She forced herself to shake that thought out of her mind before it had fully developed. Considering her aroused state, she just might take that idea and run with it.

"Perhaps I can offer you a ride?"

"Nope. I know my keys are here. Somewhere." She pulled out her wallet, which took three-quarters of her purse's interior. "Here they are!" She jangled them before him. "See?"

He swiped them from her before she knew what he'd done. His grin was downright sinful. "And now they're gone."

She shot him a mocking smile. "Cute. Now, hand them over. I need to get home. It's getting late."

He lifted them high, just out of her reach. "Only if you promise me one more kiss."

Okay, he was playing a juvenile game, but she could handle that. One good turn deserved another. He'd get what he had coming. She just needed to think quick.

Too bad her brain was on hold at the moment!

He leaned down, a goofy pucker screwing up his handsome face.

She could give him a kiss where he wouldn't expect it, and steal the keys away. Maybe. Or, she could simply give him what he wanted.

What the hell? She pressed her mouth to his.

He didn't respond. His mouth felt stiff under hers. His body remained still as a stone statue.

She pulled away. "What the hell was that?"

"I might ask the same."

"You didn't kiss me back."

He tipped his head—that was a cute look for him, innocent, like a puppy. "Well, you didn't kiss me first."

"I sure did." What was he talking about?

"That was not a kiss. At least, not the kind I was expecting from a woman as beautiful and passionate as you. It was a…a grandma kiss."

She laughed, at the grandma kiss jab, but also at the beautiful thing, and at the passionate thing. Where did he get his lines? Did he read them somewhere? Practice them in front of a mirror?

"What are you laughing about?" He crossed his arms over his chest.

That mocking grin was the final straw. By God, she'd show him! She'd kiss the hell out of him until his balls were so flaming hot he couldn't walk, and then she'd leave.

He'd be fucking a blow up doll or jerking off all night long to get rid of his blue balls!

# Chapter Five

*Throwing caution to the wind can be a hell of a lot of fun.*

"Hang on, buddy," Jane said, giddy with a sense of adventure. "You're about to find out." Completely and deliberately casting aside all sense of propriety, she reached between his legs, and with one hand stroking the stiff bulge in his pants, she reached up with the other and coaxed his head down. She spent no time luxuriating in the kiss, but went right for the good stuff. She urged him to open his mouth and thrust her tongue inside, delving, tasting, mating with his tongue.

He groaned, the sound spurring her to be even more brazen with her actions. She broke the kiss, but only long enough to look down and unfasten his pants. She slid her hand inside his snug underwear—so warm!—and fisted his erect cock. Holy shit, it was huge! Her initial impression hadn't been wrong.

That must have been his undoing. In a heartbeat, she found herself spun around and pinned against the car's hood. Hands were everywhere, exploring every inch of her body. Sliding through her hair, gripping her neck, teasing her nipples to aching points, and massaging her mound until her juices were practically pulsing out of her. There was only one thought on her mind: Fuck me. Now.

A second later, he swept her up into his arms, carried her to the black Jag parked a few spots away, and dropped her into the passenger seat. Still dazed and lost in a mire of need, she watched him drive her home.

She didn't ask how he knew where she lived. Didn't really care at the moment. All she cared about was having that beautiful cock buried deep inside her. He helped her find her keys and unlock the door, and the minute they were inside, he also briskly helped her out of her clothes—if you could call it helping.

Actually, she thought she might have heard a bit of ripping. No matter! In a strange way, it was actually stimulating.

Before she knew it, she stood before him, completely naked in the middle of the living room. Lights on—something she'd never done, even with her ex.

His gaze raked over her flesh, practically scorching it. She saw the primal urge in him. His jaw muscles tensed, his neck muscles tensed, his shoulder muscles tensed. He was visibly a bundle of handsome, jaw-dropping…need. And he'd gotten that way by looking at her. Wow!

"You are absolutely stunning," he half-said, half-growled.

She felt a smile forming. "You like?"

"Can't you tell?"

"I could tell better if you were undressed." Her gaze focused on the junction between his legs and the visible bulge in his pants.

"In time."

He stepped closer, and her body prepared for an onslaught of sensation. Instead, he halted inches from her, looked down and smiled.

"First, I want to have some fun. Are you willing to play along?"

Her mind zipped in a million different directions, but her body careened down the road that led to pussy-dripping arousal. That word. Fun. It could mean so many different things. Some scary—if he was into some crazy stuff—pain, torture, that kind of thing. She ached to find out what he meant.

"Trust me," he said into her mouth as he kissed her. The words echoed in her head. "Trust me." His tongue dipped into her mouth and he drew hers inside his, sucking it, teasing it. The similar sensation of sucking burned between her legs. He nipped her lips with his teeth, and the same nipping stung her pussy lips. Yet, his hands remained at his sides.

She needed his touch! Her pussy ached to be filled. Her muscles pulsed and twitched. Her knees grew wobbly.

As if he knew she would collapse at any moment, he swept her into his arms again and carried her back to the bedroom, running his hand along the wall and snapping on the overhead light as he found the light switch, and laying her on the bed. He pinned her there, a thick arm on either side of her shoulders, his body poised above hers. She wanted to feel his weight on her, between her legs. Not knowing what else to do, she lifted her knees and wrapped her legs around his waist.

"No-no. Not yet." He sat up and gently removed her clinging limbs. "I will tell you when. The beauty of sex is in the building need. If you hurry to the end, you miss so much."

Ugh! Her body—every frickin' inch—was screaming for completion. Take her time? She wanted him now!

"Patience, love." His gaze wandered over her form, feeling like a soft caress. Funny, how she could physically feel his gaze on her skin. "You will play, won't you?"

She needed him so badly right now, she'd agree to almost anything. "Yeah. Just please, fuck me."

"In time. Roll over and show me your ass."

That was not what she considered her most alluring asset—no pun intended. She hesitated, having always been uncomfortable with that particular part of her body.

"You said you would play." She heard the disapproval in his tone and swallowed a lump of regret. For some reason, at this moment, pleasing him was very important, more important that drawing in her next breath.

"But—"

"Turn around and show me your ass."

He wouldn't ask again. She knew it. She also knew she couldn't live with disappointing him. She did a log roll onto her stomach and waited.

He gripped her ankles and in a swift movement, slid her across the bed until her toes were on the floor and her chest was resting on the mattress.

She lay there, forehead resting on the soft coverlet, her bare ass hanging out in the breeze, and her cunt so wet she could smell her own juices.

"Your ass is perfect. So soft and smooth."

Was he blind?

"I want to fuck you."

Now those were words to appreciate. Her pussy clenched. This little teasing game was driving her nuts! "Then please, be my guest. Fuck me. Now."

"In time."

*Shit!* She'd heard that too many times already. When would it be time?

"Touch your ass."

"Do I have to? I mean, I have more appealing features—"

"Your ass is perfect. Touch it. For me."

*Perfect?* She reluctantly reached around and massaged her own ass cheeks. The skin was silky smooth, and the flesh soft. It was odd feeling her body like that. Odd and stimulating. The need deep between her legs was growing more urgent by the second.

"Part your cheeks. I want to see your pussy. Your asshole."

She parted them, and the feeling of total exposure practically sent her over the edge. Damn it! She needed a cock inside. Pronto. His cock. His hands. His touch. What the hell was he waiting for?

"Touch your pussy."

She traced circles around her folds, delving between them but not sinking into the soaking wetness within. Then she slid her finger up to her clit. Her body tensed with the first touch there, and she immediately stopped, knowing she'd come in no time.

"Roll over."

That was a welcome command. She did just that, sliding back on the bed until her whole body was resting on the mattress.

"No. Back to the edge." He gripped her ankles and pushed them up toward her chest, forcing her knees to bend and her thighs to open.

"Oh…" Talk about feeling exposed!

He dropped his head and laved her pussy, his tongue doing things she didn't think possible. Dipping, probing, flicking over her clit in a fast, steady beat. The sounds of his loving, slurping, licking echoed in her ears. The smell of her own juices filled her nose. Her every muscle tensed as she rocketed toward climax, and her heart filled with joy. She heard herself gasp.

He stopped, lifted his head, and grinned. His lips glistened. He pushed her back from the edge and crawled up on the mattress, his knees on either side of her hips, his hands on either side of her shoulders. "You like?"

"What's not to like?" she asked between unsteady breaths. "But, I'd be even happier if you'd take off a few of those clothes."

"Fair enough." He crossed his arms over his torso, gripped his shirt at the waist and lifted it over his head. The muscles of his stomach, chest and arms tensed and flexed as he moved.

Amazing.

The man was built like a god. And he was here. In bed. With her! Clearly she'd done something right to deserve this.

He chuckled, almost like he knew what she was thinking. "Would you care to do the honors?" He motioned toward his zipper.

"Absolutely." Dizzy, giddy, she sat up and unzipped his pants—hey, hadn't she done that once before?—cramming her hands inside to rest on his very large erection, sheathed in tight cotton athletic boxers. She forced his pants down over his narrow hips, trailing her fingertips over his smooth thighs to the dip at his knee. He finished the job, kicking the pants to the floor.

Next she worked the underwear. They were tight, hugged his cock and balls with all the love of a mother to her infant. As soon as his glorious shaft was exposed, she felt the twinge of her own impending climax. Hell!

She closed her eyes, shielding herself from the sight.

"What's wrong?" His voice caressed her insides.

"Nothing." She sounded like she was being strangled, even to herself.

He laughed. Then in a swift wrestling-like maneuver, he knocked her flat on her back. She opened her eyes to his hungry expression—a look so full of heat and promise, her whole body tingled. "Are you ready to be fucked?"

Was she ready? Hell yes! Wasn't it crystal clear?

She glanced down at his thick member. Shit! Would he fit? She'd never had someone so huge.

He forced her knees apart and up, until they couldn't possibly spread any wider, and then he kneeled before her. "Once I have you, you are mine. Do you understand?"

With his dick teasing her pussy, she couldn't give him any answer outside of yes. She didn't want to think of anyone else ever touching her again. She simply nodded and braced herself.

He started slowly, drawing circles over her pussy with his thick penis, mocking her by dipping, oh so shallow, inside. In and out. In and out. Circling, teasing. In no time she was breathless, overwhelmed, and damn desperate.

How much longer would he torture her?

"Say it," he murmured.

"Say what?" She arched her back, tempted to jump up, knock him back and climb on top.

"Say you will belong to me."

"Oh. Hell yes! Anything. Just fuck me."

He palmed her face. "I must have you."

"You can. Just take me."

In the next instant, her breath shot from her lungs as he thrust his thick rod inside. Pleasure-pain shot up her spine, delayed just a moment, and followed by the incredible, breath-stealing feeling of being completely filled by him. Her mind completely shut down as her senses took over. Her eyelids closed, cutting out the sight of him, yet in her mind's eye, his image remained. His tense expression filled her with urgent need.

Sounds exploded in her ears. His groans. Her moans. The sound of her own breath whooshing in and out.

He drew almost completely outside of her and then thrust back inside. Oh God! Her insides churned. Her stomach muscles were so tense they were cramping. Her foot muscles were in spasm, and her thighs opened so wide her hips screamed in protest.

Jane was in absolute heaven. Her soul danced with the stars.

"Again!" She lifted her arms overhead, bracing her hands against the wall. "Please, again."

He drew back and slammed into her again, several more times. With each thrust she reached an even higher level of tension until she feared every blood vessel in her body would burst.

He reached with one hand and circled a fingertip over her clit. Hand and dick worked in unison, circling, thrusting, circling, thrusting. His mouth plundered hers. His breath filled her lungs. She pulled him deep inside her spirit, drinking his very essence. The wash of heat flashed over her body as she soared high. Her body clenched and convulsed in a climax like none she'd ever experienced. Her pussy pulsed around his cock, and he increased the pace, slamming into her. He growled as he found his own climax, huffing loudly with each thrust as he drove his spasming cock deep inside her.

Boneless, he dropped to her side, his still erect penis buried in her twitching pussy.

"Holy shit. What was that?" She didn't know what else to say. That was the most mind-blowing sex she'd ever experienced.

So this was what all the fuss was about! There was something to the whole sex thing after all. Why hadn't she ever seen it before? In her marriage, sex had been so dull, routine.

"You like?" He looked as relaxed and collected as he might standing at a street corner.

"How the hell do you do that? I'm a quivering mess, and you look like you're ready to run a marathon."

"Swimming. It does wonders for your stamina."

"Well, thank God for swimming!"

She closed her eyes and let herself be snuggled close to him, her head cradled in the crook of his shoulder. With the taste of him in her mouth, his seed spilling from her pussy, and the steady thump of his heart in her ear, she drifted off to sleep.

As her final thoughts fed into her dreams, the words he'd spoken drifted through her mind. She was his. He'd asked her, and she'd promised.

She was his.

# Chapter Six

*Sex is like any other sport, it taxes muscles no other activity does.*

The next morning, Jane awoke alone to the dull ache of a body that had used long neglected muscles, a nearly stripped bed, and a sopping wet pussy. The smell of sex was everywhere and followed her to the bathroom as she staggered to the shower.

What a night! Had that been her? Quivering, begging for sex? She'd never believe it in a million years if she hadn't seen it for herself. She had been so out of it, she didn't remember him kissing her goodbye and leaving.

Grateful today was Saturday, she took her time showering, fully appreciating the water beating against her back, stinging her skin. She spent the day trying to keep her mind busy. She tried reading, but after her eyes skimmed the same page for the fifth time, she gave that up. She tried watching TV, but everything reminded her of Josh, and that only led to flashbacks of last night's escapade.

Even the memories of what she'd done last night made her hot. She'd done things she'd never done with anyone. She'd felt things she'd never felt with anyone. His body was so amazing. His touches were so intoxicating. His voice turned her knees to marshmallow. There wasn't a thing he asked for that she denied, right down to masturbating in front of him.

Next time, she'd do more than that if he asked.

She couldn't think about that right now! At least, not if she was going to assume it was anything more than a one-night stand. Those three words—one-night stand—made her heart sink.

Somehow, her car had appeared in her driveway in the morning, so she went shopping and bought a sexy little negligee she couldn't pass by and a couple of new bathing suits. She went out to eat—she hated eating alone—and called Diana to let her know she was still alive.

When she returned home, she waited for his call, thinking he must have her number since he'd known where she lived.

No call.

She went to bed that night with sweet memories on her mind that fueled fantasies as she masturbated. The next day she followed much the same routine, grateful when that day ended as well and she was left to relive her memories in her dreams. Monday morning, she went to work.

Her life suddenly felt empty.

At work, a flower deliveryman walked into the lobby. Could that gorgeous bouquet be for her? She signed for it. Nope.

She went home, convinced it had been a one-night stand, and even more convinced that wasn't enough. The instant she opened her door, she new the truth. There would be no more guessing.

Her living room was full of spring flowers. The heady aroma filled her nose and lifted her spirits instantly. She hopped with giddiness and giggled then slammed her door shut and reached for the closest bouquet.

*To my Love, Josh.*

Okay, so he wasn't much for words. He was more a body language type of guy, not that she'd ever complain. Although the word love was nice.

The dozen or so vases of flowers said all she needed to know: he'd be back.

That night, she masturbated with even steamier fantasies of Josh. The rest of the week passed with no further contact from him, but she didn't mind. She went to work and spent her nights at home as always. But now, unlike before, she had something to look forward to.

Friday swim class.

Of all things!

That day, Diana met her after work and they drove to class together, just as they had last week. She was more nervous than she remembered being before. She was having a hard time hiding it from her intuitive friend.

"What's your problem today?" Diana asked as she sat in the locker room watching Jane deliberate over which bathing suit to wear. It was a toss-up between a hot pink number with higher cut legs or a conservative two-piece that showed just a slice of her stomach. "Are you a basket case because of the swimming or because of the man teaching the class?"

"Both."

"What happened last week? You never did tell me, and that plain pisses me off." Diane gripped Jane's wrist. "If you fucked him, I want to hear every last detail."

"I'm not going to tell you a thing." She felt her cheeks flaming.

"You did!" Diana jumped to her feet and pinned Jane to the lockers with two hands on her shoulders. "You little… Tell me."

"Nope. I'm not kissin' and tellin'. What I did or didn't do with Josh is my business."

"I hate you." She grinned as she spoke and squeezed Jane's shoulders. "Good for you. I hope it was incredible."

"It was." The words slipped out before she could stop them. Damn it!

Diana gave her a smack in the gut. "I knew it! You aren't the little Miss Goody Two-Shoes you've led me to believe all these years, are you?" She plopped back down and yanked on Jane's wrist. "Fess up. I need to know. What happened?"

Jane tried to pull her arm free, but her friend had a grip like an anaconda. "We ate dinner and kissed in the restaurant parking lot. One thing led to another, and he came back to my place—"

"And you had wild monkey sex!" Diana finished for her, clapping her hands in approval.

"We made love," Jane corrected. Although she had to admit to herself it was as close to wild sex as she'd ever experienced.

"Bullshit." Diana dropped her jeans, slid off her thong and pulled up her bikini bottoms. "You don't know the man. It was beautiful, earth-shattering, exhausting, walk-like-you'd-been-riding-a-horse-for-a-week sex." She pulled off her shirt and unhooked her bra.

Jane diverted her gaze, catching her reflection in the huge mirror on the other side of the room. "It felt like much more. And then he sent me flowers."

"Oh. That's very gentlemanly."

"You don't understand. He sent me dozens of bouquets. My entire living room is full. One thing has me curious, though." She hazarded a glance at Diana. She was dressed—well, as dressed as a woman can be wearing three scraps of fabric. "The man drives a Jag—"

"He does?" Diana's eyes registered dollar signs, and Jane stifled a giggle.

"Yes. At least, I'm assuming it was his car. He had the keys. I suppose he could have borrowed it. Don't you know what he drives? You know him better than I do."

"I used to know him better than you do. I can't say that anymore. I've never seen him drive. He must have money, maybe even a chauffeur."

"That's what I'm thinking. But the man teaches swim classes at the Community Center. How much money could he be making?"

Diana shrugged and walked to the mirror, primping. "Maybe he's a rich guy living as a regular guy so he can find a wife who will love him for who he is—"

Jane shook her head. "You've been watching too many movies. I'm going to change. Be back in a few." She changed into her bathing suit—she chose the bright pink one-piece. The color seemed to complement her skin coloring nicely. When she returned, Diana was fully dressed again, in her street clothes. "What happened? You're going to class with me, right?"

"No. I have to leave."

"Now? Where?"

Diana headed toward the door. "I'll call you later."

"Wait a minute!" She caught her friend's arm and gave it a mighty tug. "You said you'd go to class with me. You promised."

"You don't need me here. And I just got a call from a friend—"

"It's not Mark, is it?"

Diana didn't meet her gaze, so Jane gave her friend's arm another yank. "No, you don't! That asshole doesn't deserve the time of day from you. I won't let you."

"We're just going to talk."

"Bullshit! What's there to talk about? Who he wants to fuck next?"

Diana looked stricken, and only then did Jane realize how much her friend cared for the cock-sucker. Shit! That man didn't deserve the buckets of tears Diana had shed when she'd found him sleeping with some bimbo in their bed. He didn't deserve the second round she'd showered upon him when she'd found him fucking a different woman in his car in the middle of an empty parking lot. He sure as heck didn't deserve a minute of her time, now that she'd finally quit crying over him. No man deserved that much forgiveness.

She switched gears, settling for a lower one. "Please. I love you. You can do so much better. Why are you even considering this?"

"I'm not considering anything. Now, go on. You're late for class. And don't drown. I'll kill you if you do."

She left.

Jane considered dressing and going home, and would have if she wasn't so damn anxious to see Josh. She'd have to face the lesson alone this time. All in an effort to see a man.

Did she have it bad for him or what?

Her heart thumped in her chest, and she looked down at her hands, white knuckling her towel and wringing the poor thing. Her stomach boiled, bubbling and jumping.

This wasn't good. How sexy could she look in this condition?

She went to her locker and stood there, tempted to leave, but also wanting like hell to see Josh. Why hadn't he called? If he had, she wouldn't be…

Oh… He knew. If he called or saw her, she wouldn't come to the lesson. She wouldn't conquer her fear. Had someone told him to force her to attend the swim lessons? Diana?

Damn it! She'd have to go in there and make it through the class or she would look like a fool. Still feeling sick, she walked through the locker room and entered the pool area.

He was there, standing by the side of the pool, a whistle caught between his perfect, white teeth. He smiled, and she smiled back, feeling like the most important person on earth. Every nerve ending honed in on him, and everything else in the room dropped away. She walked toward him, so eager to hear his voice…

…she fell, catching a glimpse of his wide eyes and gaped mouth before the water crashed in around her.

Sitting on the bottom of the pool already? Damn!

She pushed off the concrete, her lungs burning. Her arms thrashed, her legs kicked. She surfaced, gasped and felt herself sinking again.

Then he was there. He touched her, and her panic ceased, like magic. She looked him in the eye and heard his voice in her head.

*You could've waited for a kickboard, beautiful, but I'm impressed with your optimism.*

*This is no time for teasing, buck-o!*

He smiled, and a bubble slipped through his lips. *It's okay. I'm here. When I'm with you, nothing can happen.*

*How're you doing this? The first time I heard your voice in my head, I thought I was hallucinating. But again?*

*I can't explain it right now. Just trust me.* He palmed her face, and she almost felt safe. For some reason, it didn't matter that she wasn't breathing. That was one hell of a miracle.

He wrapped his arms around her waist and swam upward. As she broke through the shimmering surface overhead, she almost regretted leaving the secret blue world they shared under the water.

"What happened?" she asked. Dazed, not sure if she wanted to believe what she had just seen and heard, she reached for the pool's side.

"You fell into the pool." With hands cupping her ass—a convenient excuse to cop a feel, for sure—he gently helped her out of the pool, supporting her as she tried to convince her legs to bear her weight.

"I know that. But there was something else." She was going crazy! Didn't schizophrenics hear voices? Diana had a friend who was a shrink...

"You aren't going crazy." He looked across the pool at the other swimmers in the class and blew his whistle. "Okay, everyone back in the pool. I want two laps with the kickboard before session is over."

The menagerie of swimmers, mostly middle-aged women wearing those tacky rubber flowered swim caps, started across the pool toward them.

"How do you do that? You're reading my mind, aren't you?" A whole lot of curiosity and an almost equal dose of fear settled over her like a London fog. He was reading her mind? Egad! She had no secrets!

"I'm not reading your mind. I'm guessing what you're thinking. And based on your reaction, I'd say I'm doing a damn good job of it."

"Too good." She didn't know whether to be relieved and laugh off her suspicions or be worried. She decided she'd play it safe and take things slow. Of course, no sooner did she make that decision than her body made its own determination, thanks to a seemingly innocent touch on the arm.

A current of electricity charged through her body, and she hopped away from him. *What the hell was that?* "Did you just shock me?"

He looked at her with a puzzled expression, his eyebrows knitted tightly together. "No. Shock? How?"

"I felt something." Her body heated, as though that buzz had ignited a flame. The warmth traveled down, over her stomach, and between her legs. She caught his gaze and felt her pussy get wetter.

There was that fuck-me look again. *Anytime, handsome.*

Her knees turned to mush, and she needed to sit. She dropped to the poolside and dangled her feet in the water. *Ah, cool. Now, if only there was an iceberg I could stretch out on.*

He sat beside her. "After class, would you like to go out? Maybe get something to eat?"

Her heart did a little jig. "Sure, and maybe some dancing? Do you like to dance?"

He smiled—oh what a gorgeous face!—and blew his whistle. "Time's up. Everyone out of the pool." Then he turned to her. "I'm a terrible dancer, I warned you. I'm game if you are. I'll meet you outside." He stood and helped her up, leaving buzzing tingles on her skin where he touched her. "By the way..." His gaze traveled up and down her body. "...very nice swimsuit."

# Chapter Seven

*Anticipation is both a pleasure and a torture, joy and misery.*

Palming a face that couldn't get any hotter, Jane went to the locker room, shed her "very nice" bathing suit, and jumped in the shower. The locker room was quiet, and the warm water felt wonderful running down her body. As memories of that crazy moment at the bottom of the pool buzzed through her mind, she couldn't help touching herself. Her eyes closed, she soaped up her hands and lathered her breasts, teasing her nipples. His voice bounced around inside her, vibrating like her favorite sex toy between her legs. She slipped a finger inside her pussy, and her knees gave way.

Struggling to stand, she forced herself to turn off the water and get out. She'd be nuts to make Josh wait long. He was traffic-stopping gorgeous. Returning to her locker wrapped in a towel, she pulled out the snug jeans and sexy top she'd packed, just in case. She dressed in a changing room. With the help of a blow dryer and a little make-up, she was looking pretty damn good in two snaps. The whole time, she couldn't shake a giddy sense of expectation.

Tonight would be memorable—like first fuck memorable.

She slid on her shoes, gathered her things, and headed out the door, thrilled by his heated gaze as he saw her emerge from the building.

"You look fantastic." He reached for her hand and held it high. "Spin around."

She did a little pirouette, or at least the closest thing she could manage to one, giving him a little extra time to enjoy the rear view.

He took her duffel bag and growled. That had to be a good growl.

She didn't have to wait long to confirm it. After tossing her bag in his back seat, he opened her door and helped her into the passenger seat. Then he bent low and whispered, "I could fuck you right here and now."

*In a car? I've never fucked in a car! To hell with dinner.* Boy, if that collection of words didn't tempt her to can the dinner and dancing and accept his invitation, the sight of his gaze as it traveled over every inch of her barely-clad body did!

"Food first. And dancing," he said, his strong hand running up and down the car door. *If only you were stroking my body like that...* "Then we'll get to the good stuff." He winked, closed the car door, and came around the other side and started the car. "Let me have your hand."

She reached across and he caught her fingertips in his, tickling her palm with his thumb. It seemed as though the nerve endings in her hand connected directly to her pussy. She swore he was stroking her clit in that slow, teasing motion. Her eyelids grew heavy, her pussy wet, her head swimmy.

Then her hand rested on something hard and her eyelids lifted. *Oh yeah*!

Only the stick shift. Rats!

She glanced over at Josh, and his playful eyebrow waggle made her chuckle. "What do you want me to do with this?"

"Stroke it?"

She laughed. "Okay." Trying hard to make it look sexy, and donning what she hoped was a porn film starlet's best pout, she slid her hand up and down the stick. She moaned for good effect.

He laughed. "You're too much fun." The next thing she knew they were rocketing up the street. The car was such a smooth ride, she wondered if they weren't flying, hovering just above the road. Moments later, Josh parked the car in front of a seafood restaurant.

Seafood? Again? Ugh.

"I hope you don't mind coming here. I love seafood."

"Well, it would be nice to go to a steakhouse or something."

He shuddered.

The man was repulsed by the mention of a steakhouse? That was a strange reaction. She'd never seen anyone grossed out by dead cow before—unless they were vegetarian. "Why the beef about beef?"

"Can't stand it."

"I've yet to meet someone who hates beef. How about chicken?"

He made a funny face, his mouth twisted into a comical scowl. "Yuck!"

"Wow, okay." She had to admit, she'd once thought herself a little funny about food, since she tended to eat the same things all the time, but this guy took the cake—or rather, didn't take any cake from what she could see. "So, you like seafood. Anything else?"

"Nope. That's about it. A few vegetables."

"Fruit? Bread? Sweets? Everyone loves sweets."

"Nope. Nope and nope." He got out of the car and went around to open her door.

*I guess I'd better get used to seafood restaurants.* Of course, most restaurants offered some variety on their menu.

They walked hand-in-hand into the restaurant and were ushered to a quiet table in the corner of an empty dining room as soon as they stepped inside.

"Special treatment?" she asked after the hostess left them. "I'm impressed. How'd you manage that?"

He waited for her to sit before he took his seat next to her on a cozy L-shaped bench. "Well, considering I own this place, they should give me a little respect."

"Oh, really?" Now things were starting to make sense! He was a business owner. In that case, why did he teach swimming lessons? Considering what he drove, she doubted he needed to moonlight at the Community Center. "Do you like owning a restaurant?"

"I had a lot to learn when I opened my first one, but I quickly learned the value of a good manager."

"First one?"

"Yes. I own seven. All seafood."

"Wow, that's a lot of seafood. And a lot of work." She took another look around. The restaurant was impressive. Luxurious was the best word she could come up with. Tastefully decorated, not loud or garish as some places could be. Decorated completely in shades of blue, from a deep navy to the softest aqua, it reminded her of the sea. "How do you find the time to teach swimming? I mean, I always thought restaurant tycoons were busy all the time, didn't have time for things like that."

"I make time." He stopped speaking as the waiter delivered drinks and some kind of deep fried, batter-coated squiggles. He nodded a silent thank you and continued. "I like to give back to the community, and I love swimming. It made sense to teach."

This guy was a lot more than a stud—not that the stud part was all bad. Could she get any luckier! Wealthy, respectable, caring. She had the feeling she could easily fall in love with him.

There had to be a hitch. He was too good to be true, and she knew what that meant.

He was.

She had to find a fault, any fault, or she'd forever be waiting for the reality bomb to strike. She watched him down a few of the batter-coated thingies.

"Aren't you going to try some?" He offered her a morsel.

"No, thanks. My religion strictly forbids anything coated in batter and fried."

"I think you'd like it if you tried it." He waved it in front of her nose. It smelled safe enough, a little fishy but not too bad.

"Okay, a small taste." She opened her mouth and he dunked the piece in cocktail sauce then slipped it inside, licking his lips as he traced her mouth with his fingertip.

And already, before the main dish had been served, the words "fuck me hard" trailed through her mind. What would he do to her tonight? His mercury-blasting look promised plenty.

She bit down, remembering he'd placed something edible in her mouth. Not bad. A little chewy, but also crunchy and salty, with just a taste of tomato.

"Do you like it?"

"It's better than I expected."

"Would you like more?"

That question could be taken any number of ways. *Sure! Give me more of those electrified touches and pussy heating kisses. Fuck me.* "No, I'm fine. I'll wait for my salad. What is that stuff, anyway?"

As the last word emerged from her mouth, the waiter stepped forward with more plates. He set several dishes before Josh.

*Who ordered all this?* She took in the spread on the table. That was one hell of a lot of food! Crab legs, little white round things, fish of some kind. A lobster. On her plate, a mouth-watering hunk of steak and a lobster tail. "We didn't order. How'd the waiter know what to bring?"

"I hope you don't mind, I took the liberty of arranging everything ahead of time."

"Gosh. No one's ever done that for me before. I don't know what to say. Thanks, I guess." She poked at the lobster and cringed. "I don't think I'll be able to finish all this. Are you really going to eat all that food?"

He smiled at the disbelief in her voice. "You bet I'll eat it all."

"I don't know how you do it." She made her best effort at downing the steak, watching him eat like he hadn't touched a bite in years. When her stomach was simply too full to stuff another bite in, she handed over the untouched lobster, and he ate that too. "You are a mother's worst nightmare. You probably put the woman in the poorhouse trying to feed you."

He grinned. "Thankfully, where we lived, there was plenty to eat."

"Well, unless you live in the ocean, you have to pay for it. Seafood is damn expensive. I can't imagine a parent who could afford to feed a ravenous teenager crates of fish and crab legs every day."

"No." He shook his head, mirth playing over his features and giving them an endearing, youthful appearance. "We caught our food."

"Oh. So, where'd you grow up?"

"Just outside of Sydney."

"Australia?"

"No, Nova Scotia." He slung an arm over her shoulder and pulled her closer.

It felt nice, cuddling like that. Warm, and secure. She rested against him, almost forgetting what they were talking about. "Oh, I didn't know there was a Sydney, Nova Scotia."

"It's on the north-eastern tip. It's the most beautiful place. Would you like to visit there sometime?"

Wow! Was he inviting her home to meet mom? Already? "Sure." She tried hard to hide the excitement in her voice. "That would be nice. I've never been to Canada—I mean, I've been to Windsor and Niagara Falls, but that's it."

"We'll go, then. Soon." He stood and helped her out of the cozy booth. "Now, let's go dance."

Funny, suddenly she was more in the mood for a quiet evening at home. "We don't have to."

"Nope. You wanted to go dancing, so let's go. I have a friend who owns a place down the street. They play great music. I think you'll like it." He led her through the crowded dining room—the entire place was packed! A few waiters and hostesses gave them a smile and nod of recognition as they passed. She felt a million eyes on her as he guided her outside with a hot hand at the base of her spine.

The cool air outside was a welcome relief from the heat running through her body. That simple, innocent touch was stirring all kinds of thoughts, and those thoughts were raising her core body temperature by the second.

"Would you like to walk? It's just up the street."

"Sure." *Anything to cool off.* If this dance bar was anything like the ones she frequented with her friends, it would be loud, wall-to-wall with people, and unbearably hot, and hot was one thing she didn't need.

Why were they even going?

Sure enough, they stopped at a nightclub with a line of people wrapping around the outside of the building. Yet, as she'd already come to expect, they were treated like royalty and let in without a word.

The club's inside was very dark, almost too dark. Neon signs glared from every wall, directing people to the bathrooms, bar, and so forth. The interior was crowded, a sea of bodies and faces, but it seemed to part as Josh stepped in front of her to lead the way. She gripped his hand as if her life depended on it.

Somehow, they wove through the crowd and entered another room. This one was huge, black, with high ceilings and flashing lights. A sunken dance floor was below, with writhing, gyrating dancers filling every square inch of space. Some kind of techno pop she'd never heard blasted from every angle, making her ears scream in protest.

"Well? What do you think?" Josh shouted.

"It's pretty neat."

"Want to dance?"

"Sure." The music had a nice steady bass that would be easy to follow. It pounded through her whole body, thanks to the eardrum-shattering volume. She followed Josh to the under-lit dance floor where he found a square foot or so of space at the front of the floor, near the DJ's booth.

The DJ, a dark guy with some wild looking long hair, waved at Josh and shot him a friendly smile. Obviously Josh was a regular there, or the DJ was the owner-friend Josh had mentioned.

Didn't matter. All that mattered at the moment was the heavy bass thrumming through her body and the man standing next to her. Josh caught her waist, pulled her against him until they were obscenely close—not a bad thing at all, thanks to his hard-on—and started moving…

Completely out-of-sync from the music…and not at all in the smooth, dignified way he did everything else. By God, he was a bad dancer. The worst she'd ever seen.

Her heart jumped with joy. He wasn't perfect! She admitted this was probably the least of his faults—all men had a boatload—but it was the first she'd seen. For that she was grateful. His twists and jerks, grinding his pelvis into hers, which she did appreciate, only endeared him to her more.

He couldn't keep the beat if his life depended on it.

She tried to show him, tried to lead, but after a moment, she ended up following his offbeat movements, and laughing herself silly.

She'd never had so much fun! Never had she found a man who couldn't dance worth a darn so incredibly, undeniably sexy.

Her pussy was dripping wet, along with the rest of her, when they left the dance floor and made their way to the quiet darkness outside an hour or two later. The chill slapped her, stealing her breath for a moment, then seeped inside, cooling her just enough to be comforting. They walked hand in hand to his car.

*Now what?*

"Will you come home with me?" he asked.

*Thank you, Lord!* She didn't need a written invitation. "Okay, but what about my car?" she asked, suddenly remembering her car was still parked at the community center.

"I'll have it brought to my place."

What? Did he have servants, too? Now, she had to see his home. Images of multimillion-dollar palaces played through her mind. "Okay."

He gave her another of those promising looks as she sat in the passenger seat, and her body tensed from flushed forehead to wobbly knees. She toyed with the hem of her top as she waited for him to start the car.

"I don't live far." His voice was hot and silky, sultry as a summer night. Her pussy began that familiar tingle.

"Okay." She swallowed, even though her mouth was as dry as a desert. She tried to lick her lips, but there wasn't a bit of moisture on her tongue to wet them. Every muscle in her body tensed, both from the excitement, the knowledge of what was coming, but also from a bit of the jitters.

"You got pretty quiet on me. Are you okay?" He glanced at her as he pulled up to a red traffic light.

"I'm fine. Just a little overwhelmed by everything."

"Overwhelmed in a good way, I hope."

The light turned green, and as if he didn't have to look to know it had changed, he set the car into motion.

How the hell did he do those things? Talk in people's heads. See things without looking? Send bolts of electricity through her with the smallest touch?

Finally, he looked back to the road. "If you're overwhelmed now, wait till you get to my place."

"Should I run now while I still have the chance?" she half-joked.

He laughed a wicked chuckle, as hot and sexy as the look he kept giving her. The same look that was making her heart do some really interesting things, and turning her legs into marshmallow again. "Probably should," he responded, turning down a street lined with magnificent brick homes. Huge, immaculately landscaped, the houses had to run a couple of million dollars, easy.

They turned at the end of a street and followed a winding road through a wooded area. Lights twinkled ahead, through the trees. As they drove slowly up the road, a house appeared in a clearing.

A wide circular drive led up to a massive house with a deep blue painted door. Jane's car was sitting in a parking area to the left.

How did they know to get her car already? How had they started it? She possessed the only set of keys.

Besides, he hadn't called anyone, not that she'd seen. He hadn't left her sight. What was going on?

He parked the car before the front stairs. "Welcome to my home."

She glanced out the window, awestruck. She'd never stepped foot in a place like this. Evidently the restaurant business produced a pretty penny…or he wasn't telling her the whole truth.

Accepting his hand, she stepped from the car and walked up the stairs. The building was even more gorgeous up close. It was dark outside, so details were hard to see from far away. But now that she was near, she could fully appreciate the smooth stone walls, pillars and mermaid carved into the door.

As she stepped inside, she felt as if she'd traveled to the bottom of the sea. Just like his restaurant, blues and greens decorated his house. The tile floor shimmered, one-inch square glass tiles in deep blue and aqua. The walls were adorned in two-story tall murals of sea life, and the lighting was muted, soft and reflective, sending sparkles off the tiles and crystal chandelier overhead. "Wow," was all she could manage. Her throat closed tight as an oyster shell.

"I enjoy the sea." He led her up the sweeping stairs to the balcony above.

"I'd never guess."

"It reminds me of home."

"If this place reminds you of home, then I want to get my ass to Sydney tomorrow." *Or run like hell. Where is Sydney? At the bottom of the sea?*

"I can arrange that. My treat."

Taken by surprise, she looked at him. He couldn't mean that, could he? His treat? He was as serious as death. "I was kidding."

"I'm not."

Well, what does one say to an invitation like that? It made her insides a little squirmy. Warm and happy, but uneasy too. "We can talk about it later, I guess."

She followed him down a hallway, feeling like her feet were sinking into the sandy-colored plush carpet. She half-expected to hear seagulls and waves crashing.

He stopped at the end of the corridor, before a paneled door. "Before we go in here, there's something I should tell you."

*Here it comes! I knew he was too good to be true.* She braced herself for an unpleasant surprise.

## Chapter Eight

*Fear and arousal are nearly physiologically identical. Both produce dilated pupils, rapid heart rate and wobbly knees.*

Josh hesitated at the door, knowing he was about to shove gentle, bright and funny Jane into a foreign world. He wanted to savor every moment. There was nothing as erotic as introducing a new partner to his world. He had the unmistakable feeling this would be the last time he'd be doing that.

He sighed at the thought, gripped the doorknob and gave it a twist. "I have some unusual furnishings in this room, and I didn't want you to be shocked."

"Unusual? Like how?" She sounded a little nervous, not that he could blame her. He had read every one of her thoughts. Her fears of the sea ran deep and wouldn't be easily conquered. Those weren't the only fears he sensed. Still, he also saw the longing she tried to hide even from herself. The wish for things new and exciting. The hope for love. The need for a challenge. She would appreciate what he was about to do in no time.

His pants grew a little snugger at the picture of her showing her gratitude, in a most sincere way… "Um, like I was saying, I have some unusual furniture. Think of it as my playground."

"Sounds…interesting."

He opened the door, not surprised by the gasp he heard to his left. He caught her wrist before she made it more than a couple steps back down the hallway.

"Are you a nut? My God! I should have known. I've been telling myself you were too good to be true all along, but this…!" She stabbed her finger in the general vicinity of the room. "This is too much. I'm outta here."

"Please. Stop. Listen." He forced himself not to use his power over her mind. He hadn't needed it all evening, and for some reason, that made a difference to him. She was there of her own free will. "It's not as bad as it looks."

"Sure, buddy. And what might I find in there?" She pointed at the floor to ceiling aquarium. "Are those sharks? In your bedroom."

"Maybe, but they can't hurt you. The tank is completely water tight—"

"Sharks aren't sexy. They're ugly, and scary, and mean. Shit!" She yanked harder. "I should have listened to my own reservations. What is with you and the ocean? The murals on the wall and ceiling look so…real!" She wrung her hands. "Heck, if not for the bed, I'd think I was standing on the bottom of the sea. It even smells like the sea in here. Let me guess…" She walked to the bed and pushed on the mattress. "Gee, what a surprise! A water bed."

"What are you so scared of?" He knew the answer, but he wanted to hear her speak it.

"Water, for one." She took another shy glance into the room again. "Hadn't you noticed I'm a little nervous around water? That tank belongs at Sea World, not in someone's bedroom. Do you have a whale in there too?"

"Only a small one. Please trust me. The water will stay where it is. The sharks and whales too. I want to cherish your body, not destroy it."

"There is no way in hell I'll go in there. Making love with a bunch of sharks and fish watching is plain creepy." Her words were firm, but her tone wasn't. It had softened a touch, and that was more than a little encouraging.

If there was one thing he knew, it was how liberating facing one's biggest fear could be. Jane Wilde could use more than a little liberation. Yep, she'd be a quivering mass of appreciation in no time.

He stepped into the room and shed his shirt, grateful for the caress of cool air on his skin. He'd been wearing clothing daily for a long time now, months, in fact, so he figured he should be used to the scratchy, heavy, confining feeling, but he wasn't.

"It isn't going to work." She didn't take a step away.

He shed his pants. What else would a guy do?

"Yeah, yeah. You're sexy. So what? So what if you're built like a frickin' god? I'm still not going into that…in there with that ocean of water."

He pulled off his shorts, his erection tightening his pelvis muscles as he watched her gaze settle there. "I know you enjoy my body. Come on in. Let's play. It'll be an adventure. I know you want to explore the forbidden. I know you're curious. Be honest with yourself."

"I am being honest." She poked her finger in the direction of the door to his secret room. "What the hell is in there?"

"You're not quite ready for that…yet." He took her hand and led her inside then closed the door behind her. "Trust me."

"Trust? No way."

He pulled her inside. "I know the mix of fear and excitement is making you hot. Your pussy is getting wet. Your heart is thumping in your ear."

"It is not."

He knew she was lying. The scent of her juices was driving him insane, but he forced himself to remain sedate. He changed subjects. "Have you ever wanted to be tied up?"

"Not in relation to sex."

What other kind of tying was there? He didn't ask. "Doesn't it make you hot thinking about losing control?"

He felt her shudder—and it was a good kind of shudder, he might add.

"Losing control makes me think of adult diapers," she said reaching out to touch the heavy glass tank wall. She no sooner made contact with its cool surface than she yanked her hand back.

She was no easy customer, but he was enjoying the verbal swordplay. It was all part of the game, a part he enjoyed as much as any other. If Jane was as adept at the other parts—and he knew she was—this would be one hell of a night.

"How about a nice, safe, hot bath?"

"Now, that sounds nice. I can handle a bathtub full of water."

He led her to the *master* bath—he loved that term!—and relished her sigh of appreciation.

"This is amazing."

"You like?" He tapped the button on the wall and the Jacuzzi tub filled with churning bubbles. Steam drifted into the air. "Now, it's always best to take off your clothes before you get into a bath." He spoke to her shallower parts of her mind, knowing he wouldn't need to go deeper.

She was ready.

His cock reared up in response.

"Undress for me, love," he whispered.

Jane couldn't believe herself. She was still here, in this place, with that huge aquarium practically filling the next room. Despite the fact that the décor made her feel as if she was one hundred leagues under the sea, she didn't want to leave. Everything he'd said had been true. She wanted to be fucked silly, and the little bit of fear underlying her desire only made this whole thing that much more erotic.

Josh cleared his throat and commanded, "Take off your clothes. And don't remove your eyes from my face while you strip."

Her insides tingled as she watched brain-melting desire play over his features. She quickly kicked off her shoes, took off her shirt and jeans then worked her bra clasp, catching it before it slid off her breasts.

Holy shit! He looked like he'd devour her, literally. And she was ready to come already.

"Off with the underwear. I want to see all of you."

She let her bra drop off her arms then worked her underwear over her hips. She felt so naked, but it was a good feeling of exposure, a sexy feeling. Her pussy muscles clenched and her heart skipped in her chest, hopping around like a rabbit.

"Nice." He nodded with appreciation. "Turn around. I love to look at your ass."

She did as he bid, eager to spread her legs and show him everything. Her knees were as wobbly as a newborn baby's. She felt herself sinking to the floor.

"No. Stand up."

She locked her knees against the urgent need to drop.

"That's it, baby. Now, spread your legs for me. Do you know how much I love looking at you?"

Oh, yeah! That was a step in the right direction. Naked, her legs spread as much as she dared, considering they still had to hold her up. Weak and wobbly, and wanting to lie down and pull him on top of her, she braced herself by gripping a towel bar and forced herself to remain standing.

A soft touch, tickling soft, at the back of her knee nearly sent her falling to the floor. But a firm grip on her thigh kept her upright. His touch, which left a trail of goosebumps the size of Mount Everest in its wake, meandered over her legs, skipped the sensitized flesh between her legs, and landed at the base of her spine.

Her back muscles flexed and her ass jutted out.

Josh growled. The man was a beast, and she loved it!

The tickly thing ignited every nerve ending in her back and neck then slipped down her spine and disappeared. She turned her head. "You stopped?"

"Time for your bath." He took her hand and led her to the tub and she stepped in, shocked by the nearly scalding heat of the water.

She got no further than ankle deep before she yanked her foot out. "Shit! That's hot."

"It's good for you." He lowered himself into the water until only his waist and above was visible. "Please tell me you aren't afraid of a little heat."

"I'm not. I mean, within reason. I don't like to get burned."

"No one does. Look. I'm in here with you. We'll both be burned."

For some reason, that didn't make her feel any better. She found the double entendre interesting, stimulating, even if the literal subject wasn't so enticing. She gave the bath another shot and stuck her foot into the water. This time, it didn't sting as bad, and so she moved slowly, easing her body in up to her waist.

"See? It's comfortable—a few degrees shy of being unbearable." He sunk lower and pulled her to him.

His hands resting on her waist sent energy zapping through her body, and her senses came alive. The water's scent. The bubbles dancing over her skin. The anticipation of his next touch.

He steered her around until she was facing away from him then pulled her onto his lap. His erection stabbed her ass, and she shifted herself to accommodate it, rotating her hips and then rocking them back and forth and running her ass up and down its pulsing length.

Josh groaned, gripped her hair and tilted her head, licking, tasting, nipping her neck. A chill shot down her spine, despite the furious rise in her body temperature. She rubbed her ass harder until he gently lifted her up.

"If you don't stop that, I'll come. And I'm not nearly ready to do that." He gripped her shoulders and eased her against him again until her back pressed against his chest. He gently pulled her legs apart so they rested on either side of his, and she sighed at feeling so open to him. "Now be a good girl and sit still. I'm going to wash you." He plucked a bar of soap from a basket and lathered his hands then ran them down her stomach and up over her breasts.

*Oh... This is better than chocolate, any day.* "Wash me good. I need it." She closed her eyes and savored each touch, the way his fingertips teased and pulled at her nipples, pinching, tugging, driving her insane. Without thought, she arched her back, thrusting them out for him.

He slid his hands down again and she waited, anxious to feel those fingers between her legs. Wet, hot, slippery. Instead, he ran them down her hips to her thighs, his stomach pressed firmly against her back, his upper arms resting against the outside of her breasts and pushing them together. "Look at this body. It's perfect. Absolutely perfect. Tell me it's mine."

"It's yours."

"For always."

Did he really mean that? Did she want him to mean it? "For always."

He stood and scooped her out of the tub. The air felt freezing cold as she emerged from the thrashing, steaming water, and she clung to him, seeking warmth. Thankfully, there was plenty of that.

He carried her back into the other room, the one with the aquarium that would dwarf the one at the zoo. He left that room behind—thank God!—and carried her down the hall to the next room.

Her heart rate slowed about fifty beats per minute, still faster than normal but much better, when she saw the four-poster bed swathed in blue satin. Now, this was more like it!

The satin was silky smooth against her back as he set her upon it, cool and soft. She sighed, with both relief and pleasure.

"Don't get too comfortable yet."

That warning didn't go unheeded. She sat up. "What does that mean?"

"Shush, Love. No need for fear. I'm going to make your wildest fantasies come true." He walked to the closet and opened the door.

Holy shit! What was that? There weren't clothes in there that was for sure.

Lots of black leather, whips, stuff she couldn't begin to describe or name hung on the back wall. She didn't see a stitch of clothing.

For a brief instant, she considered leaving. This was all too much. Josh was clearly into some heavy-duty stuff, whips, chains…

He turned around, a steel bar in his hands and two wide bands wrapped around his upper arm. He almost looked like a hero from one of those low budget sci-fi movies. Her pulse quickened, from both fear and anticipation. It was an intriguing sight.

"Don't worry. It won't hurt a bit. You'll thank me."

"Won't hurt?" What was he going to do with a metal bar that wouldn't involve pain? "I'm having a hard time believing that." She scooted away from the edge of the bed.

"I know your fantasies." He crawled onto the bed and kneeled before her. "I know your deepest desires, the ones you won't even admit to yourself."

She felt her face heating. Could he really know? No! That was impossible. He was just playing. It was a game. "How could you possibly know that? And I don't remember ever fantasizing about something that vaguely resembles a curtain rod." But she could almost admit she was curious. "What does it do?"

He slid the wide bands off his biceps, and here she'd thought they were part of a costume. Too bad! He clipped them on the loops on either end of the bar and held the whole shebang out for her to see. "It's a spreader."

"A spreader? Um. I'm almost afraid to ask this. What does it spread?"

"Your legs."

"Oh!" An A-bomb exploded between her legs. That was kind of exciting. She reached out and touched the metal cuff. Soft material lined the inside of the metal. Okay. So maybe this could be fun. Her pussy was sure voicing its approval.

"I'm going to strap this on you." With a palm on her breastbone, he forced her onto her back. Then he wrapped a cuff around her right thigh, and as he parted her legs to secure the second one, a warm, steady throb settled between them.

This was fun!

"Now what?" she asked, heating up as she watched his gaze crawl ever so slowly over her body, resting between her legs.

"Now, I secure your hands."

"Okay." She couldn't believe she was playing this game! But it was exciting. More than exciting, it was exhilarating, like a trip down a dangerous, thrashing river in a blow-up raft. She'd never toyed with danger before.

She liked toying with danger, she realized as Josh kneeled over her, his gorgeous erection inches from her nose as he strapped her wrists onto a second spreader hooked to the headboard.

She lifted her head and licked his cock, savoring his scent and taste. Pure heaven! Look at that stomach! It was right out of a Calvin Klein ad. And those thighs... Everything about his body screamed sex appeal. She ran her tongue down his erection and nuzzled his balls.

He growled and moved out of her reach—damn him!

"It's my turn." He smiled.

She liked the hint of devil in that smile. Curious, anxious to see what would happen next, she watched him. He shifted his weight slowly, every minute movement seemingly intentional. His cock brushed by her mouth, and she lunged forward to try to taste it.

"No-no. I said it's my turn. You lie still." He lifted himself on hands and knees, corded muscles in arms and shoulders flexing into delicious lines. She swallowed.

He dropped his torso lower until his skin was a hair's breadth from her breasts, and she arched her back to make contact.

"I said lie still."

She flattened her back.

"You must play the game by the rules." He lowered his face until his mouth nearly touched hers. "Don't move, or you will pay the consequences."

His nearness was torture enough! What more consequences could she pay...then again, her thoughts raced back to that closet full of contraptions. She supposed he could come up with more than a few alternative forms of torture.

She let her eyelids drop closed, intending to focus on her other senses. First, she drew in a deep breath through her nose, and was rewarded by the minty smell of his breath, the floral scent of the soap on her skin. The sound of his breathing in her ear, made her squirm. Tiny hairs all over her body stood on end in reaction to his nearness.

It was a heady, intoxicating mixture of sensations, and in no time, she found herself lost in them. Then he pushed her thighs up high, toward her chest. She was exposed! Open to him. Damn did it feel good!

The first touch to her pussy was a light one that sent a wave of warmth through her whole body. The muscles in the soles of her feet contracted, and her stomach tightened.

"You are so beautiful. Look at you, so wet and ready for me. Do you want to feel my cock inside?"

She nodded.

"Speak to me, love."

"Yes."

"Yes, what?"

"I want your cock buried deep inside of my pussy." Those words sounded strange coming from her mouth. She might have thought them over the years, but she'd never spoken them. Never had talked dirty in the bedroom.

"Not yet."

She wasn't sure she could take any more teasing. Maybe he was waiting for something. "Please?"

He chuckled. "I appreciate your asking so politely, unfortunately it's not good enough."

"What more could you want? Do you want me to beg?"

"Yes."

She opened her eyes, first catching a good long look at her legs, knees bent, thighs spread wide. It was almost enough to make her climax. "You're kidding, right? I mean, I'm open as can be here, wet as the ocean, and you want me to beg?"

"It's not your fault you're not ready yet."

"How more ready can a woman be?"

"Plenty. Now, if you want to find out for yourself, do as I say. Close your eyes."

She dropped her head back and closed her eyes.

Another touch started at her inner thigh, slowly creeping up to the juncture between them, skirted her folds and then meandered down the other leg. That was enough to get her stomach muscles pulsing. She lifted her hips a little to open herself to him more, silently pleading for his touch on her clit. Her pussy was achingly empty, pulsing, wet, needy.

Then he touched her, drawing an oval over her folds, dipping low to her puckering asshole before climbing to her clit. Her inside muscles tightened, eager to feel his fullness within their walls.

"That's it, love. I want you wet for me."

What the hell had she been before? She could feel a trickle running down her crack. Her whole body was in tune to his touch, tensing and releasing in a slow, sultry tempo.

"I want to taste you." His tongue teased her clit as a finger plunged inside.

That was the end of her! Her thighs strained, eager to spread wider. Her whole body heated. She moaned, trying like hell not to come. The irony of that situation didn't go unnoticed, even though her mind was swiftly leaving her. How many times had she faked an orgasm in the past?

She could barely contain herself. "I need you to fuck me," she heard herself murmur as she lifted her head to look at him.

Had she just said that?

"What?" He raised his head, his mouth moist and oh so tempting. She could smell herself everywhere.

"Fuck me."

He licked his lips, and she tasted herself in her mouth. "Seems to me you're in no position to make demands."

"Please?"

He smiled. "That's more like it. But if I fuck you, what will you do for me?"

"Fuck you back?"

He clucked his tongue.

What the hell? What red-blooded man considered fucking an insult? She was spread wide, soaking wet, and begging for sex. What more could the man want?

"What will you do for me?" he repeated.

"What would you like?"

"Your complete submission. You will do as I say."

"What have I been doing?"

He tipped his head and raised his brows in a silent challenge.

"Okay." At this point, she was so hot, she'd agree to just about anything—even climb Mt. Vesuvius, if she had to. "Fine. I'll do whatever you ask."

"Excellent." He kneeled between her knees, and she tensed with expectation. "I want to watch you touch yourself."

Had she just heard him correctly? "Um. I can't exactly do that." She tugged on her bound wrists to illustrate. "Did you want me to try to escape?"

"Nope. I would rather release you myself." He unstrapped each wrist, kissing each one. "Now, I have given you pleasure. Will you do as I ask?"

"Touch myself like this?" Knowing full well what he meant, but wanting to tease him, she ran her hands over her stomach and breasts.

"No, touch your pussy. Show me how you masturbate. I want to watch. I want you to share your most secret fantasies."

He had to be kidding. She waited for him to admit he was, but he merely nodded in encouragement. So, feeling a little self-conscious, she ran both hands down her body and over her mound.

"That's it. Show me your slit."

She parted her puffy lips and ran a fingertip around the perimeter.

"Where do you touch yourself? How? What do you think about? What do you see when you close your eyes?"

She closed her eyes and tried to concentrate. Her favorite fantasy was a bit weird, and she'd never told anyone. "I start slowly, my legs open like this, and I trace slow, soft circles over my clit."

"What do you think about?" He wasn't going to let her keep any secrets? Not even the deepest, most intimate ones?

"I…I haven't told anyone."

"You promised complete submission."

"I know. But…" She had, dammit! "Okay. I imagine I'm in a far away place and I'm being tested by a tribe of people. They want me to mate with their leader, but I must prove myself. I must come in front of them. They're watching me."

"Very nice."

His cock plunged inside, filling her. Brilliant colors shot through her mind. Her entire body contracted into a tight ball as heat burst from her center and spread outward.

With each thrust, she felt the tingle of her impending climax. Closer, closer, hotter, hotter. Her senses closed in on themselves as her eyelids fell shut. Sounds echoed through her body, bouncing, vibrating, roiling like waves. Josh growled, and his voice blazed down her spine like lightning as he repeated her name.

She gasped and tasted tangy salt on the air, as if they were by the seashore. She gripped the sheets in her hands, and the bedding fell away, sifting through her fingers like sand.

Oh…

Was she lifting into the air? Floating? Had her soul left her body?

"We are one now," Josh whispered, his body joined with hers. His hands gripped her thighs, his fingertips digging into her flesh. "We are one soul. One spirit. Forever."

"Forever," she repeated. She screamed as every part inside clenched and then pulsed, rocketing her into the heavens.

"That's it, love. Prove yourself to me."

Her pussy milked him, the pulsing going on for an eternity as he slammed into her over and over again.

Then he cried out with his own ecstasy, and drove himself deep inside. She felt his body tense against hers, then he dropped on top of her, and as her body relaxed, she opened her eyes.

Her mind froze at the sight before her.

He was different. His skin had taken a distinctly ashen shade.

Holy shit! Was he dying or something?

# Chapter Nine

*When a loved one turns gray before your eyes, there is reason for alarm.*

Damn! Jane's eyes were wide as saucers, and he had the sneaking suspicion it had nothing to do with fucking.

He glanced down. Shit. The transformation was beginning again. His skin was dry, gray. He needed to leave. But what excuse could he deliver after having made love to her, after pushing her so close to her limits?

"I have an allergy," he said, hoping she would believe him.

"Are you sure that's all it is? You look…terrible."

"I'm okay, but I'll need to get some medicine. I have to leave." He released her legs from the spreader, then stood and went to the room's second closet for his robe. No sense scaring her more. The transformation would happen quickly. She didn't need to see any more.

"Can I drive you somewhere?"

"Nope. I can manage. It isn't life threatening, just a little strange looking."

"But—"

"I know it's rude, but you should probably leave. I'm so sorry, love. I hate to fuck and then shove you out the door." He took her into his arms and her body clung to his. He loved the feel of her curves, soft and supple. He loved the woman who possessed them, too. "I meant everything I said earlier. Someday I'll explain it all to you. Will you trust me?"

The problem was, what would she—a human who lived in fear of water—do if she learned he was a selkie, a being tied to the sea for eternity? How could he tell her? How could they live together? He had to return home. His people needed him. He had obligations. This visit to the land dwellers was for only one purpose: to mate.

She couldn't possibly come with him…or could she?

Shit! He needed time to think. But first, he had to return to the sea, return his body chemistry to normal. Living among the land dwellers had its dangers, among them pollution.

He felt himself growing weaker. "I have to leave. I'm very sorry, love. You do believe me, don't you?"

"I can see something's wrong with you." She wrapped a sheet around her body and glanced toward the hallway. "Okay. Where are my clothes?"

He punched the call button, summoning his butler. The man appeared within a heartbeat, Jane's clothing folded and stacked neatly in a bundle. Without a word, he handed them to Josh and left. Damn good service.

"Again, I'm sorry to do this. I'll call you in a day or two. Promise."

She wiggled into her snug jeans—no panties, nice!—and skimpy top, then sat on the bed to slip on her shoes. "It's okay. You can't help it." Her gaze traveled over his face. "You really look bad. You're getting darker. Are you sure you'll be okay? Maybe I should call nine-one-one."

"I'll be fine. Please, don't worry." He ushered her to the door, gave her a reassuring kiss, and watched her drive away. Then, not bothering to dress, he jumped into his car and headed for the shore. No sooner did he touch the water than his legs fused, his feet thinning to become fins. He took several deep breaths, filling his blood with oxygen, and dove under the surface.

Of all the days to be forced to return to the sea, why did it have to be midnight Fridays?

He descended into the cold waters, his body rejuvenated by the swim. It would take him a full twenty-four hours to combat the damage it had endured in the past week. His heart ached knowing he would spend it without Jane.

As he reached a nearby ridge, formed from ancient underwater earthquakes, he neared a gathering of friends, fellow selkies who had similarly been summoned to the surface for mating. Among them was his closest friend, Max.

*I smell mating,* Max said telepathically, immediately sending the rest of the group scattering to the four corners of the earth.

*You could smell mating if it occurred a hundred miles away.*

*Who couldn't? It's a damn pleasant scent. So, I assume you've bedded that little beauty I saw you with last night? Details, man. Give me details.*

*You're not getting a word.*

*Killjoy. Why are you so secretive? You've always shared.*

*This is different.*

*It is? How? Fucking is fucking.*

*That's what you think.*

Max gave him a playful jab in the shoulder. *I have to admit, I'm a little jealous.*

*You mean you haven't had any luck? You? The fucking machine of the Atlantic? I can't believe it!*

*I still have a moon's full cycle yet. I'll find my mate. Don't you waste a second worrying when you could be fucking. So, how do you find it with the land dwellers?*

*Intoxicating.*

*You're smiling.* Max scowled and circled him, swimming slowly, like a shark. *In fact, if I didn't know better I'd think you like it a lot more than you should.*

*You wait. You'll be wearing a shit-faced grin after you find your mate.*

*Nope. Not me. I prefer our own for recreation.*

*There are benefits to fucking outside of water.*

*It's not the venue, it's the partner. I can't see a land dweller being more fun than a female selkie. Humans are so stiff and reserved.*

*You're talking shit. You don't know.*

*I've seen. Even the ones who are obviously looking to mate run squealing when I proposition them.*

*Well, what do you say to them?*

*'Let's fuck?'*

Josh laughed, knowing his friend probably said just that, he was so tactless. *You have to woo them.*

*Bullshit!* Max tossed a dismissive hand. *I don't want to go through all that just to fuck. Why can't they be more up front about it? Why must we play such asinine games?*

*You're an ass.* Josh shook his head. *The games are half the fun.*

Max knocked on Josh's forehead. *Hello? Is this the guy who left home vowing to bed the first land dweller he came across, no fanfare, and return home? You've changed your tune, buddy.*

*I have not. I'm still singin' the same tune. Just changed the notes. Believe me. The games are the best. Use what you have, delve into her mind and uncover her fantasies, and you'll be singin' too.*

*I can't believe I'm hearing this from you.* Max swam away. *Next thing you'll be saying you love her…*

*I do.*

Max spun around, sending the cool water rippling from him in all directions. *You do? Shit! You know the rules. You can't bring her down here. She can't know.*

*There are exceptions.*

*Bullshit.*

*I am king.*

*Correction – you will be king. Your old man is still firmly seated on the throne.*

*As future king, I'm free to choose my bride.*

*Why the hell would you want one of those? They only drag you down. Plus, none of our kind has married a land dweller for eons. Mating is one thing. Marrying is another.*

*Maybe it's time to change that. I've never believed there should be a difference.*

*I disagree, but outside of that argument, how're you going to convince her to live down here? To the humans, this world is hostile. They lack the adaptations we have. Can't hold their breath, can't handle the water pressure –*

Josh shrugged his shoulders. He'd already thought about those things. *That's not as big an issue as you think. A little bit of genetic engineering, a marrow injection, and she'll produce the protein necessary to store oxygen in her blood as we do –*

*That isn't exactly a safe procedure – or a pleasant one. How will you convince her she must go through with it? Hell! How will you convince her of what you are?*

*She may have her suspicions already.*

*You let her see you during the Transformation?* Max's eyes widened.

*Not completely.*

Max merely shook his head and swam away. One word rang through Josh's head as he watched his disapproving friend's back fade from sight, *Fool.*

*I'll show you who the fool is, my friend.*

* * * * *

"How was swim class?" Diana, driving her fire engine red Mazda, poked Jane in the ribs.

Jane leaned to the right, out of the line of fire. "Fine."

"Are you dating that guy officially yet?" Carmen asked from the back seat. "Or are you just fucking him?"

"Carmen!" Diana scolded, shooting her a warning glare in the review mirror. "Of course she's just fucking him, aren't you, Jane."

Jane watched her two friends swap looks—Diana's scolding, Carmen's clueless—and laughed. "She can ask. I know you're both dying to hear all the ugly details."

"And the not so ugly ones, too," Carmen added.

Diana smiled. "Okay. Answer the question, Jane."

"I don't think anything is official yet, but he's throwing out some hints. I'm pretty sure he expects this to be an exclusive thing."

"Did he spend any money yet?" Carmen asked.

"Just bought flowers."

"Oh." Carmen responded flatly.

She turned around to face Carmen. "It was a shit load of flowers."

"I'm sure he'll do better than that," Diana added obviously trying to sound encouraging.

Now she was feeling backed into a corner. "We had dinner." *At his restaurant where he didn't have to pay the check.* "And he's...done more than that. He had his servants drive my car home..." She let her voice trail off, annoyed by the judgmental looks on her friends' faces. "It's not about money, you two."

"Since when?" Diana asked, giving her a taste of the scowl that had formerly been reserved for Carmen. "We've always said we'd only date guys who were one: loaded. And two: willing to spend money on us."

"He's loaded," Jane acknowledged, hoping to dodge her friend's tongue-lashing before it really got going.

"Then he's just a tightwad?" Carmen asked.

"No—"

"The man says he wants an exclusive deal," Diana interrupted.

Oh boy, she was in for the inquest. Why had she even told them as much as she had? That was just plain stupid. "No."

"But that's what you just said," Carmen piped in.

Shit! First she got the sex of her lifetime, only to be hurried out before her core body temperature returned to normal, endured over twelve hours of silence when her phone should have been ringing off the hook, and finally forced to endure another Saturday night with the girls.

Granted, this time they'd opted for going out instead of vegging in front of the TV, but she was about as thrilled to be clubbing tonight as she would be facing a blood transfusion.

There just had to be a better way to spend a Saturday night! Add to the seemingly cold indifference Josh was showing her after tossing her out earlier, the endless stream of criticism volleyed her way since she'd taken a seat in Diana's overgrown roller skate, and she was fit to be tied.

"If you two don't lay off, I'm going home."

"What's up with you?" Diana scrutinized her as she waited for a traffic light to change. "Granted, you're always a little bit of a wet cloak, but tonight you're downright depressing."

"Well, don't let me ruin your night out. I told you. I'm tired."

"Had a night of wild sex, did you?" Carmen teased.

"Yes," Jane said, feeling herself getting seriously steamed. She'd make them shut up for good. "Involving whips, chains and spreaders."

"Oh..." Carmen sighed.

Diana laughed. "You? No way."

"How would I know what they're called if I haven't used them?"

Diana shrugged. "The 'net. There are dozens of places with that stuff on there."

"And why would I do that?"

"Morbid curiosity? Although I have to admit, I admire you for even going that far. There is something to it. You should try it sometime."

"I just told you. I have!"

Diana rolled her eyes. "I love you like a sis, but you're pathetic."

"I'm pathetic?" She felt herself seething, and before she could stop herself, she blurted, "And what did you do yesterday with asshole?"

"Nothing. We had something to talk about."

"Yeah, yeah. Like what lingerie to wear before you fucked, the black teddy or the red baby doll?" *Score two points for me!* She chuckled at her own joke.

Carmen laughed.

Diana didn't laugh. "Ha ha. Very funny. Sorry to disappoint you both, but we didn't sleep together."

"Then what was that all about?" Jane asked, now truly curious. "One minute you were in a bathing suit, ready for swim class. The next minute you were dressed and running out the door."

"He needed some advice."

*No way!* "From you? Come on. Since when did he start listening to anything you have to say?"

Diana pouted. "I do know a thing or two about a few things, thank you."

"I know," Jane conceded, sensing her friend's feelings were getting hurt, and not liking the fact that she was the one doing the hurting, even if Diana was being nasty. "But he was always complaining about you being such a bossy bitch. And now he asks for your advice?"

"He never said that." She parked the car in the club parking lot, and Jane looked around.

They were here, again? Did Diana know she'd come to this club last night? She studied Diana's face.

"What?" Diana snapped, looking as friendly as a crocodile.

Guess she didn't know, or didn't feel like talking if she did. "Nothing."

"This place is new. I thought we'd check it out." Diana flipped down the vanity mirror and double-checked her hair. "It looks promising. Check out the guys at the end of the line."

"Maybe the guys do. But the line doesn't," Carmen pointed toward the stream of people wrapping around the building.

"No problem." Diana said, smoothing on another coat of lipstick the same shade as her car. "I'll get us in."

Jane smiled at the memory of walking hand-in-hand with Josh, getting the red carpet treatment, dancing with him, her body pressed to his.

"Earth to Jane..." Carmen, standing outside Jane's open door, snapped her fingers in front of Jane's nose. "Are you coming in or staying here?"

"You mean I have a choice?"

"No." Diana shoved her out the door. "We're in this together. Let's go."

Jane fought back a sigh and shuffled along between her friends. She couldn't count the number of other places she'd rather be—including a dentist's chair, or even Josh's aquarium room.

In fact, that room with all those bizarre fish was holding more appeal with every minute that passed without her hearing from him. At least she'd be there with him, and she'd know if he was okay.

Diana walked past the line of people and waltzed right up to the doorman.

This was going to be good. Jane knew every one of Diana's tricks, and she had the sneaking suspicion none of them would work.

"Hi," Diana purred as she approached the man who vaguely reminded Jane of Goliath. He was plain huge.

"Hi. Would you please take a place in line, Miss?"

Diana giggled and placed a dainty hand on her mostly bare chest. She looked over her shoulders, as if she had no idea who he was speaking to her. "Surely you're not speaking to me."

Goliath nodded and smiled.

Diana rested her hands on her hips and leaned forward just enough to make her skimpy top bunch around the neckline, flashing him a nice view of her rack.

Diana was one class act.

Goliath wasn't buying. He didn't even take a peek. Not a brilliant man. What man would turn down a free shot of tits?

"Sorry, Miss, but the line's back there. If you want to step your pretty little foot in this place, you're going to have to do what everyone else is doing…wait."

"Well!" Diana snagged Jane's elbow with her own. "I can't believe this." She stomped back to the car.

"But aren't we going inside?" Carmen asked, trailing behind Diana and Jane.

"Not on your life. I don't wait. For anything. Get in." Diana took her seat behind the wheel and started the car. "I'd rather watch *Splash*…again. Come on, girls. Let's go home."

There was a God!

# Chapter Ten

*Yes, the quiet ones are the ones to watch out for.*

"Your turn." Diana pointed at Jane.

Jane, being her usual self and not particularly thrilled with the party game Diana had chosen, responded with, "I'll pass."

"No way." Diana pulled Jane off the comfy couch and shoved her toward the chair—more inquisitions! Where were the spotlights?

"Okay." Jane sat and sighed, knowing she'd never leave The Chair until she fessed up. "The kinkiest thing I've done during sex was get tied up. It was a lot more fun than I thought it would be."

"You really did that?" Carmen asked, looking awestruck. "You?"

"Yes, me."

"Well, you go girl!" Diana leaned forward. "Details, please."

"No, way." Jane crossed her arms over her chest.

"I can't believe it, our little Jane." Diana hugged Carmen's shoulders. "She's growing up."

"Oh, for God's sake, give it up. I didn't don leather and whip the man."

"Why not? That's fun too. Did he ask you to?" Diana toyed with her hair. "You know, if you ever need that sort of thing, I have a—"

"What was it like?" Carmen interrupted.

*Thank you, Carmen!* Every now and then she did something brilliant. "Very exciting…and a little scary. He had these metal rods, tied my hands and feet—"

"Oh, my God!" Diana jumped up, her hands cupped over her mouth. "He's into bondage? I mean really into bondage? Josh?"

"Yeah, I guess. If that's what that means. I don't know. It's not like he has a torture chamber or anything, though." *Maybe a torture closet.*

Diana dropped back onto the couch. "I'm green with envy."

"You are?" That hadn't been what she'd expected to hear.

"He likes to play. You'll have a hell of a sex life from here on out if you stick with him. Damn!"

"Sorry." She figured she should apologize, for some reason.

"For what?" Diana smiled. "This is exactly what you needed. Don't you feel better already?"

"Better? Than what?"

Diana shook her head. "You know. More liberated. Free to enjoy sex. To explore."

"I guess." She thought back to how she'd felt immediately after their last night together—before he'd shoved her out of the house. "Yeah. I guess it's okay doing naughty stuff. I had no idea being a bad girl was so much fun."

Diana jumped to her feet. "See? There you are!"

Carmen stood up, went to Jane and gave her a hug. "My new hero!"

"Okay, okay. That's enough." Diana pried Carmen from Jane. "What are you doing tomorrow?"

"Who? Me?" Jane asked, wondering where Diana was going with that question.

"Both of you."

"Well, I have to do some grocery shopping, but that can wait, I guess," Carmen said.

"I don't know." Jane tried to create a good excuse in a hurry, but came up empty-handed. "I guess I don't have anything going on."

"Good! We're going shopping, girls. Tomorrow. At that fancy new mall across town, then we'll grab some lunch. Now…" she said as she motioned toward the door, "…out, out! I need my beauty sleep, it's late, and my refrigerator is empty."

Jane was not about to argue with Diana on this one. She was glad to go home, even if it meant she's spend the next eight hours or so tossing and turning, and wondering if Josh was okay. Why hadn't he at least called her to let her know he was alive and well?

She drove home and went to bed, and as expected was tortured by memories of Josh. The way he touched her, the sound of his voice.

Man, she had it bad!

The next morning, sleepy and sore, she got up, did her normal morning routine and met up with Diana and Carmen for their shopping trip. They drove to the mall, Jane dodging both Diana's and Carmen's requests for more details about Josh. Their first stop in the mall: the lingerie shop. Why did that not surprise her? They picked out a racy red number for Jane, and Jane shelled out the cash—quite a huge hunk, she might add—for it. Some treat! They headed down to the next shop. As Jane passed a jewelry store display, a gorgeous ring caught her eye, and she went inside to get a better look at it.

The center stone, square cut and not too terribly big, was the color of a tropical sky. Absolutely stunning. Clear twinkling diamonds rimmed all four sides. The whole shebang was set in platinum.

The salesman approached. "Magnificent, isn't it?"

"Is it a sapphire?"

"No. It's much, much rarer. I'm selling that ring on consignment for a friend. It's a blue beryl stone. Have you heard of it?"

"Nope." The only thing that convinced her she wasn't getting a line of shit was the setting. Who in their right mind would set a stone less than worthy in platinum? "Blue what?"

"Beryl. To my knowledge, the stone is found in only two places, Brazil and Canada. It is extremely rare."

"And how did you get this one?"

"The owner also owned the mining company that discovered the stone in Canada."

"Just for curiosity's sake, how much is the ring?"

"I'm asking thirty thousand."

"Wow!" She staggered back a step. "For that? It's not even that big."

"For the kind of stone, it's very large, and quite delicate."

"Well, thanks." She turned to leave. No sense talking to the man another minute. The ring was way beyond her means. As she stepped toward the mall, and searched for her friends who had wandered away, she spied the one human being she'd kill to never see again.

Her ex. Greg Hastings.

And what was that clinging to his arm? Malibu Baby?

He smiled, and her gut tied into a knot. She hated that triumphant, rub-your-face-in-it grin.

"Didn't anyone ever tell you, messing with climbing nightshade is dangerous?" she asked, sure the joke would fly right over his head, and probably Barbie's for that matter.

"Huh?" He shook his head. "You're strange, Jane. What are you doing out here? The trailer park is south, about ten miles."

Jane ignored his jab at her working-class neighborhood. If it weren't for his parents' hasty departure to hell, he wouldn't be living any better. In fact, she knew Mr. Hastings, the pride of his country club, was spitting distance from being homeless. "Good to see you again, too. And speaking of working class taste, what happened to your last trophy? Did she lose her court case?" She smiled at the clinging vine wound around his elbow and nodded. "I'm the ex-Mrs. Hastings, in case you haven't figured that out." She offered her hand. "Good to meet you."

The woman couldn't be a day over eighteen, wore clothes so tight they resembled plastic wrap, and had clearly paid more than a few visits to a plastic surgeon. "Paula. Good to meet you, too. It's always nice to put a face to a name."

Jane bit back a nasty retort—Malibu Baby didn't know what she had coming to her, no reason to punish her more—and turned to her ex. Karma would take care of it for her. "So, are you shopping for, another engagement ring? What'll this make for you? Five in as many weeks?"

Okay, so maybe she was dishing out a little punishment to them both, Paula because she just looked too damn good wearing clothes that should emphasize her imperfections, and Greg because he deserved every bit of hell he dished out.

She glanced at Paula, not surprised by the shock on her picture-perfect face. In truth, she was doing the bimbo a favor. No doubt about it, Paula figured she was about to snag a rich husband by hooking up with a legendary Hastings. Problem was this one was piss-poor broke.

"No." He tugged on his companion's arm and turned away, saying over his shoulder, "Time to head back to the ghetto before you start absorbing some class, Jane. You wouldn't want to ruin the low class image you've got going for you now."

"You wouldn't know low class if it was fucking you."

Paula spun around, nearly knocking herself off her stilettos. "Hey!"

"No offense," Jane offered.

Greg patted Paula's ass. "At least she knows how to fuck. She doesn't lie on her back, spread her legs and take a nap like some people."

"Well, maybe I was bored because you don't know what the hell you're doing." There. He deserved a verbal kick in the balls.

"Patty here doesn't have any complaints—"

"Who?" Paula asked, her eyeballs bugging out of her head.

Oh, boy! He'd done that one to himself. Jane didn't bother hiding her grin. This was getting interesting. Quickly.

"I meant to say Paula. Let's go take a look at those rings."

"Who is Patty?" Paula asked, pulling away from him and crossing toned arms over an ample silicone-enhanced chest.

"It was a slip of the tongue. I don't know anyone named Patty."

Jane prepared to explain. "Patty was—"

"Stay out of this, Jane, or I'll cut off your alimony."

"She doesn't need your money anyway," a deep voice said behind her. "The pittance you could scrape together wouldn't keep her in rags."

It couldn't be Josh... Here? How?

She turned around. It was! Her heart jumped in her chest and her face heated. "Hi."

He smiled at her, his eyes warm, his gaze caressing. "Hello, love." Then he pulled her to him, tucked her hand into his elbow and turned his attention back to Greg. His expression turned downright scary. "Don't you ever speak to Jane that way again."

Greg smiled. "Oh, yeah? Who are you?"

"Jane's fiancé."

Fiancé? Had she missed something? How had she forgotten a proposal? She glanced down at her left hand, just to double-check. Nope. No ring.

Greg's shit-eating-grin faded just a touch as he gave Josh a thorough once-over. That look of male appreciation and defeat was worth every minute of hell she'd lived through when they were married. Thankfully, Greg knew power and money when he saw it. If there was one thing that Josh's personage screamed—outside of raw sex appeal—it was power and money.

"Congratulations," Greg muttered.

"Thanks," Jane said, smiling so big she felt her cheeks might crack. Lie or not, this was fun!

Greg glanced down at her hand and his cocky grin returned. "No ring? It's not official until you put the rock on the lady's finger, buddy."

Shit! Greg had always been so slick. She'd never been able to get one over him.

"We're about to take care of that." Josh glanced down at Jane, his expression so damn genuine, she was tempted to believe what he said. "Weren't we, Jane? Didn't you tell me about a ring here that you wanted me to look at?"

How did he know? How could he? "I did see one over here but—"

"Great!" Josh interrupted. He slid an arm around her waist. "Let's go take a look."

Now, she had a million questions, but she didn't dare breathe a word of them in front of Greg and Paula. Instead, she simply said, "Okay," and followed Josh's gentle lead back into the jewelry store.

"Now, which one was it again?" Josh asked. He smiled at the salesman. "My fiancée was looking at a ring a while back. I'd like to see it."

The salesman returned his expression, nodded, and practically ran to retrieve the ring. "A fine, fine piece. Worth much more than I'm asking."

Josh took the ring from the salesman and studied it. "Blue beryl. Very nice, Jane. You have excellent taste. Expensive, but I agree, worth every penny. It's exquisite."

Jane peeked over her shoulder, catching Greg's scowl. She couldn't believe Josh was going to this much trouble just to put Greg in his place. But she was sure enjoying it.

"Excuse me, sir," Greg said after a moment. "I'd like to see the finest ring you have in this store, please."

Paula's nearly six foot frame just got another couple of inches taller.

"The gentleman is looking at it at the moment, Sir," the salesman said. "Can I show you something else?"

"No, that's fine. I'll wait."

Josh slid the ring on Jane's finger. A perfect fit! It felt so incredible, and a bit scary, having something so beautiful, so expensive…and tiny…and fragile on her hand.

"We'll take it."

What? Josh didn't just buy that ring, did he?

"But—"

Josh raised an index finger to her lips, cutting off her argument before she'd really gotten going. "Hush, love. I want you to have it."

"But we're not—"

Josh looked at her with such love and kindness, her heart swelled. "We're not what?"

She glanced down at the gorgeous ring. Outside of a house, she'd never owned anything worth so much. What if something happened to it? What if she lost it? She should lock it away…

"I won't let you do that. You must wear it. Always. And think of me."

"Jane! There you are!" Jane spun around just in time to catch Diana's puzzled expression. "What are you doing?" She smiled at Josh. "Hi, Josh. What are you doing here? Just tell me you're spending money on my dear friend, and I'll be happy." And then she looked at Greg. "And him, too? My God, woman! Who else did you invite to the party?"

"I didn't invite Greg," Jane explained. "He was here, and I bumped into him. And then Josh showed up."

Carmen dropped her eyes. "What's that on your finger?"

Feeling her face blazing, Jane lifted her hand. "Oh, it's a ring."

"A ring? Like an engagement ring? You're wearing it on your left hand!" Carmen took Jane's hand and inspected the ring from every angle. "A sapphire?"

Jane shook her head. "No, a blue beryl, whatever that is."

"Is cash okay?" Josh asked the salesman.

"Cash?" Jane repeated. Who the hell carried around thirty thousand dollars in cash?

"Well…I, uh… Oh, my." The salesman stammered. "Yes, sir. That will be fine."

Josh pulled out a wad that would put Columbia's drug cartel to shame and started counting out thousand dollar bills.

Jane had never seen a thousand dollar bill. Who was the president with the funny mustache?

Josh handed her a bill and whispered, "Grover Cleveland. Keep it."

"What a joke!" Greg scoffed. "Tossing around cash like it's nothing. Sorry, buddy, but I'm not impressed."

"You don't have to be. The only person I care to impress is standing next to me." He didn't miss a beat as he finished counting out the last few bills and handed them to the salesman.

Jane turned back to Diana and Carmen, catching a silent inquisitive look between them.

Diana cleared her throat. "So, are you ditching us now that Mr. Moneybags has shown up?"

Diana sounded pissed. Jealous? Now, Jane felt like she was in the middle. She glanced at Josh, wanting to spend the rest of the day with him, but also feeling guilty for ditching her friends.

"No, you go with them. I'll see you later." He kissed her nose, patted her ass, and gave her a sexy smile. "And make sure to wear that sexy number you bought earlier. I have plans for you."

*How did he do that? How could he know what I bought?*

Her whole body heated, juices started flowing, and various body parts started tingling, especially those between her legs.

"Okay," she breathed the word more than said it.

He handed her the small jewelry store bag with the velvet box for her ring. "Go ahead and take this home. But don't you dare take off that ring."

"Okay." She took the bag from him. As her fingertips brushed his, a zap shot between them, static. She jerked her stinging hand away, dropping the bag. "Oh." She bent to pick it up, but Josh caught her shoulder.

"Allow me." He scooped it up and handed it to her again, and she took a firm grip. "I'll call you later, say seven?"

"Okay." She stopped moving. Breathing became impossible as she caught his glance. In the depths of his eyes, she saw so many things, beautiful deep blue places with shimmering lights.

Diana grabbed her other arm and gave it a tug. "Wake up, Sleeping Beauty!"

"I'm awake." Jane shook her head, waved goodbye to Josh—taking special note of the way his jeans hugged his firm ass—and turned around. Well, maybe she was a little out of it. But wouldn't any woman be after having her boyfriend show up out of nowhere—just as she was battling her ex-husband, to top it off—buy an engagement ring worth more than her car, and then run off, promising an evening of sex?

"What did you do, call him from a pay phone?" Diana asked, walking toward the main mall. "We've been looking for you for ages."

"I was going to ask you the same thing." Jane peered down at her left hand again. "I don't know how he found me. And Greg—"

"Holy shit!" Greg's voice bellowed from inside the jewelry store. "Thirty fucking thousand?"

Jane smiled. Today was going to be a very good day. And tonight...well, after this, she couldn't wait to see what Josh had in store for her.

"So, are you really engaged?" Carmen asked.

"I don't know." Jane glanced at the ring again, half-expecting it to be gone, faded like a dream.

"Don't know?" Diana gripped her hand and waved it in front of her nose. "Well, considering you just accepted a ring worth more than a year's salary, you'd better figure out what it means. Have you lost your mind, Jane? You haven't known the man for more than a couple of weeks."

Jane didn't know how to explain. "I know, but it just seems so right. Outside of the water thing—he has a fascination with huge aquariums that scare the piss outta me—we just seem to click."

"Well, before you get stuck, you'd better do some checking." Diana suggested, checking out a set of mannequins in a store window. "Make sure everything is on the up and up. Now, that's a sharp outfit. Let's go in here."

"He's your friend. You mean you don't know that?"

Diana scowled. "He isn't my friend. He was just a hunk who wouldn't give me the time of day. I thought you might like him. But I never expected…" Diana motioned toward Jane's hand. "I never expected you to get engaged in a week."

"Neither did I," Jane said, looking down into the blue stone. It looked like Josh's eyes, sparkling and deep. "Neither did I."

# Chapter Eleven

*It is amazing how heavy and intimidating a tiny stone on your finger can feel.*

As promised, Josh called at seven on the dot, and no more than fifteen minutes later, he was at her door, a smile on his face and a huge bouquet of flowers in his fist. Jane was thrilled beyond belief to see him. Positively giddy. But she needed to find out exactly what the rock on her hand meant before she started picking china patterns.

Josh handed her the flowers, gathered her into his arms, and dropped a kiss on the top of her head. "Where do you want to go tonight?"

"Maybe dinner? Nothing too complicated. I have to work in the morning."

"Perfect." His hands worked magic. Caresses up and down her sides seemed to draw the stress out of her body. He tangled his fingers in her hair and tugged, and she dropped her head back. Seconds later, her whole body tingled as he kissed and nipped the sensitive skin on her neck. Her legs turned weak and rubbery. Ready to fall to the floor, she leaned into him, but that only made things worse. With his body firmly pressed against hers, her mind had to work extra hard to stay functioning. "Oh…"

"Ready?" He lifted his head, set her back on her feet, and smiled like a playful boy. "I'm starving. Let's go eat."

She mentally kick-started her brain and heart—both of which had failed several minutes ago—and followed him to the door, stopping to grab her purse and keys.

The minute her gaze took in the vehicle in the driveway, she froze. "What is that?" Okay, she knew what a limo was, but...but why was it in her driveway? What was the special event?

"It's a limousine, love. I wanted to go all out for you tonight."

"My gosh, I don't know what to say." Her tongue felt much too thick to fit inside her mouth, and her throat was so dry she started to hack.

"Are you all right?"

He looked concerned—how sweet of him! "I'm fine. I just need a drink."

"There's champagne in the limo." He took her hand and led her to the car, stepping back to let the driver open the door for them.

She thanked the driver and bent over to duck inside. "Wow." She'd once been in a limo, years ago. Prom night. She didn't remember that limo looking as gorgeous as this one. It was absolutely stunning—for a car. She sat. Nice. Soft cushions. It smelled good, too, as soft music played from hidden speakers all around her. "I could get used to this. Can he come back tomorrow and take me to work? I might not mind getting caught in morning rush hour if he did."

Josh chuckled. "You're cute." He pushed a button. "Rayford, Miss Wilde would like a ride tomorrow—"

She clapped a hand over his mouth. "I was kidding! Oh my God, what would the girls in the office say if they saw me come out of this thing…?" Actually, that might be fun. "Okay. Carry on. I'd love a ride. But only this once."

Josh smiled and finished with Rayford. Then he took out the champagne and glasses. "Do you still need that drink?"

"You bet I do." She accepted a tall flute full of clear bubbly champagne. "What are we toasting to?"

"To a lifetime of happiness." He lifted his glass and she touched hers against it.

Guess he meant that whole marriage thing.

"Oh." He smiled wickedly. She'd come to appreciate that expression. "And a huge brood of children."

"Brood of children?" *What exactly did that mean?* "Is a brood like a gaggle, or a pair?"

"A lot."

"Like how many?"

"Oh, I don't know. Maybe ten? Twelve?"

Her head started spinning. Did he actually say ten kids? "Are you trying to kill me? Holy shit! Can women produce that many babies and live?"

He smiled over his glass and sipped. "Of course they can. Wouldn't you like to have my children?"

"Of course I would. I'd be proud to—" She would? Had she just said that? She'd always vowed she'd never have kids. "But-but ten? No one has ten kids anymore. I mean, except for farmers who need cheap labor."

He motioned toward her glass. "Aren't you going to drink to our toast?"

She sipped. Yum! Cold, bubbly, crisp. That champagne was very tasty, and she was not normally a fan of champagne.

"I'm willing to compromise, then, if you're overwhelmed with ten. How about eight?"

"Two," she countered.

"Seven?"

"Three."

"Six?"

"Five. And that's my final offer."

"Done!" The most amazing smile spread over his face, and she wondered what she'd just gotten herself into. "I'm going to be a daddy. Can we start tonight?" He waggled his eyebrows.

*Five kids? Am I nuts?* She laughed. He was so playful and funny. A big hunk of a boy, in some respects, yet commanding and protective, and sexy. Perfect. "You forgot one thing. We aren't married yet."

"That's no biggie. We can take care of that with a quick trip to the courthouse tomorrow—"

"No way! I've been dreaming about my wedding day since I played house with Jimmy next door. My first one wasn't exactly the one of my dreams."

"Lucky guy!"

She giggled and gave him a playful smack on the shoulder. "We were five. And I'm not getting hitched again at the ratty old courthouse." Wait! What was she saying? Was she really going to marry Josh? Just like that? She'd always criticized people who rushed into marriage, and there she was contemplating marrying a man she'd known for only a couple of weeks. She was nuts. Pure and simple. *Time to visit a shrink and get some good drugs.*

"You'd be nuts to turn me down."

"My, aren't we full of ourselves?"

"I'm everything you've ever dreamed of."

He was right, but she wasn't about to admit it. "How would you know that?"

He leaned forward until his mouth was a fraction of an inch from hers. "Because I know you. I know your most secret desires and fantasies. I know your dreams."

Her eyelids drooped until they closed out the world. She waited, breathless, for his kiss. He knew her dreams? He sure seemed to.

"Like now. I know you want me to kiss you, but I'm not going to. Not yet." His hand rested on her breast, and she arched her back into his touch. A fingertip teased her nipple through her snug knit top. "And I know you want me to fuck you. But I won't. Not yet." His first hand still taunting her breast, his other dropped to the hem of her skirt and slid under it, brushing over her mound and tickling the point where it met her thighs.

Her body was a lump of aching, tingling need in two breaths. "Oh, Sweet Jesus!" Had he said he wouldn't fuck her? Teasing bastard!

Kneeling on the floor before her, he used two hands on her knees to part her legs. "You love it when I take command in bed. You love to lose control. Open to me."

Her skirt hitched high up on her hips, sliding out from under her ass as her legs spread. She felt the cool air on her soaking lace panties.

"Very nice. You're wet and ready for me, aren't you?" He lifted her ankles, setting them on his shoulders. The feeling of exposure, of being so open to him only made her hotter and wetter. If only he'd fuck her!

"Please."

"Please what, love?" He rimmed her pussy with a teasing fingertip, running up and down each side while avoiding the one place that ached for his touch.

"Fuck me."

"No, no. I told you. I won't do that yet." He kissed the inside of her thigh, and she squirmed. He tickled the back of her knee, and she giggled, struggling to pull her ankle out of his grasp. He ran his tongue up her leg then down the other, and she moaned in breathless agony.

"You're driving me crazy!" She struggled to suck in a breath, knowing her brain was becoming oxygen-deprived. The world spun and tipped, and she grasped for something to steady it.

"Crazy, eh? That's exactly what I'm trying to do." His free hand lifted to slide under her top and pinch her nipple, and when he pulled, she arched her back, pushing her breast into his hand. "Do you like that?"

"Oh, yes! Very much." As a reward, she received a firm squeeze.

Setting her feet on the floor, he pulled her nipple into his mouth and suckled. "And this? How does this feel?"

"Oh…" She couldn't think of words to describe it. His voice alone hummed through her body like some kind of strange energy, lighting mini-blazes everywhere. "More."

"And what about this?" He nipped the inside of her thigh then blew a current of cool air on her hot pussy.

"Oh…" She sighed. But the brief relief wasn't enough. In fact, it only stirred added heat. "More!" Blind with desperation, she clawed at everything within reach. Every muscle in her body coiled tight like a viper preparing to attack. Shit! She craved relief, needing it more than her next breath. Her body thrummed with need, climbing steadily toward orgasm, despite the fact that he hadn't touched her pussy yet. "I'm going to do something rash if you don't fuck me. Now!"

"No, you don't want to do that."

"Why not?"

He didn't answer. Instead, he slipped a shoe off her foot and tickled the sole of her foot.

It was the strangest sensation. She felt a buzzing, zapping electricity shoot up her leg and settle over her pussy. Like the buzz of a vibrator. It hummed through her body, loud in her ears, stealing her breath, making her pussy throb and clench as if he held a vibrator on her clit.

Without warning, she jetted over the edge, her body convulsing with a powerful orgasm that left her gasping for air and dizzy. "Oh my God!"

As soon as she was able, she opened her eyes.

He still held her foot in his hands, and he was smiling. "Did you like?"

"What did you do?"

He held up his hands, palms facing her. "Everyone has energy in their bodies. If they learn how to channel it, they can use it."

"I have never felt anything like that." It was real. She'd felt it. She'd come. Hell, her pussy was still tingling. From a touch to her foot. Why her foot?

"There are nerve pathways in your body. And the one that leads to your sexual organs is here." He touched the same spot on the center of her foot. Immediately she felt that tingle again. "I believe acupressure and acupuncture use the same principle."

"I've never had those. Hell, I've never had an orgasm from someone touching my foot, either." She found her glass, which she assumed she'd set down, she couldn't remember, and took a big gulp.

"I'm hoping that will be one of many firsts we share together."

"I'll toast to that." She raised her almost empty glass and touched it to his then she downed the rest.

The car stopped.

She glanced out the tinted windows and pulled her skirt back down over her rear end. She slipped her feet into her shoes. "The beach? We're at the beach?"

Josh sat next to her and grinned. The door opened, and she stepped out onto the sidewalk. Josh followed her. "I hope you don't mind. I thought a picnic would be nice."

She looked up and down. It was a beautiful stretch of land. A driveway led up to the sandy beach, turned back on itself and headed out to the main road somewhere out of sight. A copse of trees skirted both sides of the drive. "What is this place?"

"A private beach."

"Where's the house?"

"There isn't one. Just sand and surf." He took her hand, and she followed him, enjoying the soft sound of water lapping the shore and the smell of salt in the air. In awe, she turned around completely, enjoying every sight, smell and sound. Gulls shrieked overhead, dipping and soaring over the water, and the sun hung low over the horizon kept company by pink and purple clouds.

It reminded her of that first time, the sensations she'd felt when they'd made love.

"This is breathtaking."

He led her to a dining canopy set up on the sand, just shy of the tide. Lanterns fringing the underside of the tent lit the interior, and the rich smells of food drifted to her nose on the breeze, making her mouth water.

She sat in a chair, the kind cushy you'd never expect to find on a beach, before a magnificent polished wood dining table and waited for Josh to sit. "I don't know what to say. This is amazing."

"I'm glad you like it."

"I can't believe you went to all this trouble for me."

"Why not?" He took her hand and dropped a kiss on the back. "You're worth it."

"It's so romantic. I didn't think guys knew how to be romantic." She watched the waves roll toward them. "Although the water's a little scary."

"It's out there. We're here. It can't hurt you."

"I know." She smiled as a thought dawned. "Oh my God! I get it. You didn't do this to be romantic. You're still trying to make me comfortable around water. You sneaky son of a..."

"Is that a crime? Your fear has frozen you for far too long. Isn't it time to conquer it for good?"

"Don't tell me you're going to drag me in there." She pointed at the ocean, panicking. Her heart shifted into double-time.

"No." He leveled his gaze at her. "Trust me. I won't force you. You will only do what you're ready to do. Besides, our food is getting cold. Let's eat."

She nodded and watched as he lifted the silver covers off the dishes, revealing a wide variety of seafood—gee, what a surprise—vegetables, and—thank God!—pasta. She watched in awe as Josh packed in a truckload of food and forced herself to eat a few bites.

"How do you do that?" she asked, mentally weighing the volume of food he had just consumed. It had to be somewhere near a ton.

"Do what?"

"Eat so much? I've never seen anyone eat like that."

He shrugged. "I have a healthy appetite…for many things." He grinned.

That was one expression she couldn't miss. Her body responded, warming from head to toe.

"How about we go for a walk?" He stood and took her hand, pulling her up to him.

"All right. Just don't take me any closer—"

"How about we just walk along the water's edge. It's warm tonight."

Oh boy! He wasn't going to give up easily. "How about we walk over there?" She pointed in the opposite direction.

"In the swamp?"

"Swamp? I thought it was woods."

"It's much nicer here, don't you think?"

"Not exactly." The water slid up the sand and licked at her ankles, and she jumped.

"Look at me."

She couldn't help raising her eyes to his face.

"You can do this. You are strong, capable, and have made great strides in swim class. Water is not dangerous. It's a beautiful, essential element. It heals and protects."

His voice resonated through her whole body, easing her panic and relaxing her knotted muscles. "Yes."

"Now, follow me. We're going into the water. Together." Walking into the sea, he pulled her.

She slipped off her shoes and tossed them onto the beach before following him deeper into the ocean. The water that had been ankle deep pulled at her calves then her knees. Yet she remained calm. The water felt cool and invigorating, and Josh's hand around hers was reassuring. She took several more steps until the water pushed at her thighs and looked out over the wide expanse of shimmering water. Her wet skirt clung to her legs. "It's quite pretty, isn't it?"

"Beautiful."

"I see why you like it so much."

"Love?"

"Oh yes. You love the sea."

"No, I love you."

She turned and looked into his eyes. "You love me?"

"Yes. With all my heart and soul. Be my wife."

*He loves me? He loves me!* "I want to. I mean, I accepted the ring." She glanced down at the gem that reminded her of a tropical sky. "But I thought we'd take some time to get to know each other better before—"

"This weekend. Marry me this coming weekend."

"So soon?"

"I must have you."

She saw the fierce need in his eyes, but she didn't trust herself. Was she doing the right thing? Was she thinking straight? Wasn't it insane to marry a man after only two weekends? "I…I want to."

He hooted and swept her into his arms, kissing her with such passion, the world around her dropped away. His tongue traced her lips then plunged deep into her mouth to stroke and probe. She kissed him back with equal fervor, suckling his tongue as if it nourished her. Her body tingled, heating as if set ablaze…

And then it cooled.

She opened her eyes.

Water. Everywhere. She opened her mouth, but instead of air, water filled it.

She tried to scream.

Josh covered her mouth with his and filled her lungs with air. Then he palmed her face and forced her to meet his gaze. *You are safe, as long as you are with me. Trust me.*

He spoke directly in her head, his voice humming inside, bouncing around and zapping along nerve pathways. How the hell did he do that?

*It's a skill we all have.*

*We who?*

*My…family. You will meet them next week at our wedding.*

*Just tell me we'll be married on dry land.*

His chuckles bounced around in her stomach, tickling her insides. She felt herself relaxing.

*Swim with me. We can explore. The ocean is a glorious, beautiful place.*

*We don't have any gear. Don't people use snorkels and flippers?*

*We don't need them. We don't need clothes, either.* He lifted his shirt over his head, chest, stomach and arm muscles bunching and flexing. That was a glorious, beautiful sight. More beautiful than the ocean.

Next, he shed his pants and underwear. Then he helped her out of her clothes.

There was something very provocative, very sexy and exhilarating about swimming in the buff. The water felt like silk against her skin, cool and soft. And watching Josh swim, watching every muscle on his body work, was enough to kick start her hormones.

That first erotic twinge shot from between her legs.

*That's it, love.* He slid a hand down to cup her ass, and probed between her cheeks with a finger. She arched into his touch, willing him to explore deeper.

His other hand wrapped around her back as he pulled her up against his hard form. Her breasts flattened against his broad chest and her head dropped back as he bit and kissed her neck.

Damn! She was hot. She wrapped her legs around his waist, appreciating her weightlessness in water, and kissed him, drawing in another deep breath and filling her lungs, her whole being, with his essence. As he plunged his cock deep inside, she was complete, thoroughly filled.

Her pussy closed tight around him as he slid in and out, slowly, deliciously. Her eyelids dropped closed as she clung to him, digging her fingernails into his flesh. Her mouth sought his, drinking, tasting, breathing. Her muscles tensed, her legs spread farther apart as she soared closer to climax.

He pulled out just before she reached that magical crest and led her from the water. Dazed, she followed him, unable to think of anything but completing what they'd started deep below the shimmering water's surface.

He led her to the dining tent and pulled the tablecloth off the table, and then led her to a flat rock. His hands and mouth teasing, nipping, pinching anything they came in contact with, he spread the cloth over the rock and eased her onto her back.

Her ass sat at the very edge, and she almost feared she'd fall. But as he pressed her thighs up and apart, all was lost to her but the feel of his mouth on her pussy.

His tongue lapped her folds, licking, delving into her slit, flickering over her tight bud and sending shards of light through her body. She was on fire! She needed the sea again.

He knelt in the sand and in one firm stroke buried his cock deep inside. The head struck her deepest regions, and she moaned. Teasing her pussy, he pulled out before filling her again.

Her legs opened wider as she sought to take him deeper.

"Touch yourself." His words cut through the haze of pleasure.

She lifted her hands to her breasts and teased and pinched her nipples.

"Your pussy. Touch your pussy."

She dropped a hand to her mound and a fingertip brushed against his cock. Her pussy muscles clenched, sending another wave of warmth through her body.

"Touch yourself for me." His voice sounded breathless, urgent. She could no more deny his request than stop breathing.

She sought her clit and drew circles over it, meeting the pace of his thrusts.

"Oh, yeah. I love the feel of your juices, the scent, like the sweetest perfume. Come for me, love. Drench me in your sweet juices."

She quickened the pace of the circles, as her body steadily climbed toward orgasm. Josh's fingers blazed over her skin, leaving burning trails behind them as they traveled from one breast to the other. He pinched her nipples, and she bit back a shout of pleasure. Then he kissed away the sting, leaving her nipples tight and eager for more.

The sound of his mouth working on her breasts burned into her mind. The scent of him, of sea and salt and sand, filled her nose and drifted inside her like a soft breeze, cooling the fiery furnace threatening to engulf her mind, body and soul. The taste of his lips lingered in her mouth, washing away the taste of fear and indecision until she knew she was where she belonged. With Josh, the man she loved. The man she would never stop loving.

"Josh."

"Yes, love."

"Is this for real?"

"Yes, baby. It's all real." He kissed her, his tongue working slowly through her mouth, drinking from her, savoring her. She slid her tongue into his mouth, too. There was no sweeter taste than this! There was no moment in time more beautiful as this one. There was no place more special.

She broke the kiss and sighed, content, on the verge of orgasm, her body both coiled tight and relaxed. "Thank you for bringing me here."

"Thank you for coming." He slid his cock out and then with a swift jab punctuated his sentence. "Now. Come for me."

That was all the invitation she needed. Increasing the pressure on her clit until she felt the telltale flush of orgasm rocket through her body, she sought the only place where sensations and emotions blended. The one place where her soul was free, and where she could truly be one with Josh. She gasped as her body spasmed, her pussy pulsing around his wide cock.

He groaned low and fucked her hard, thrusting deep until he found his own release, and took flight with her, howling into the night as he pumped his seed deep inside.

They danced in the air, among the stars, dipping and soared, and then fell back to the earth.

As she lay on the rock, the cool night air slowly drawing the heat from her body, and the twinges of her climax subsiding, she felt the sea's soothing waves slip up over her until she was completely immersed again.

# Chapter Twelve

*The truth is damn scary sometimes.*

She was his. There was no doubt, and regardless of the dangers, he would find a way to live the rest of his days with her. He admired her strength as she allowed the water to overtake her again. She'd done it, conquered the worst of her fear.

Because of that, he was one step closer to taking her to his watery realm. There were only a few more details left to complete, the worst being he had to tell her the truth about himself. He knew how difficult that would be. Like other selkies, he'd been told how humans reacted to being told about their world. He would likely face Jane's laughter…or worse, her rejection.

He would die.

He shook aside that thought and led her from the sea to the waiting car, wrapping her lovely, shimmering body in a blanket. In silence they rode to his home. Yet, with Jane, even the silence was comforting. The sight of her shrouded in the fluffy blanket and her wet hair streaming down her neck and over her shoulders left him achingly hard. Again.

Aware that his appetite for sex ran toward the extreme, he didn't know if he dared approach her for more lovemaking.

But when he walked her to the door and led her inside, immediately shedding the towel he'd wrapped around his hips, her appreciative gaze on his cock left him wondering whose appetite was greater, his or hers.

He smiled, his face heating. "Would you care to go to bed?"

"Only if you'll be there."

This was a woman after his own heart! Thanking the gods for their generous blessing, he took her hand in his and dashed down the hallway to his room.

This time, as they entered, she didn't gasp and cower at the sight of the massive aquarium. Instead, she lay on the plush carpeted floor, spread open, welcoming him.

A sight to behold for sure!

He fought back the urge to plunge deep inside and rush toward completion. Instead, he forced himself to go slow. He sat beside her, running a finger up and down her torso, starting at the base of her throat, running down the valley between her breasts, and circling her belly button before returning to her throat.

Her eyelids slowly closed and her hips tipped up, beckoning his touch to her pussy. Still he concentrated on going slow. It was too soon. Both their bodies needed to build energy. Even outside of the water, he could see her energy had drained away, diminished to almost nothing.

He set his mind, concentrated on the cells in his palms and left them hovering over her heart. The tingle of electricity started in their centers and fanned out before filling the air between his hands and her skin.

She sucked in a gasp as the first zap jolted her, and she opened her eyes.

"Relax and enjoy," he whispered, still concentrating on regulating the current.

Within an instant, she became comfortable and relaxed with the constant feed of energy. "That feels wonderful. How do you do that?"

"Shhh, love. Just take it in. Don't talk."

She smiled and drew from him until she had her fill. When he broke the connection, she opened her eyes. "What was that? I feel so...so good. Like I've slept a week."

"I have special cells in my skin. They produce electricity."

"Sure you do." She chuckled. "It's one of those healing things. Wait! I think I've heard about it. Doesn't it start with a K?"

"I don't know what you're referring to."

"You're funny."

She sat up and smiled—damn that was a lovely smile. He would never live another day without it. That thought brought a similar expression to his face. He crossed his legs as he sat on the floor. "Mirror me."

She sat similarly, and his gaze dropped to the juncture between her thighs. His cock reared at the sight of her pussy, the inside lips already glistening with wetness for him.

He closed his eyes, forced thoughts of fucking her aside and instead focused again on his hands, holding them out in front of his chest. "Do as I do. Put your hands up near mine, but don't touch them."

He felt his skin tingle with the electric charge, and then felt the needles of energy zap through the air.

She jumped.

He opened his eyes and watched her expression change from mild indifference to shock to awe. Tiny blue bolts of electricity jumped between their hands as he discharged energy into the air.

She pulled her hands away, studying them. "How do you do that? I've never seen such a thing. And...I won't tell you what it's doing to my pussy." Her face flushed a sexy shade of pink.

He inhaled deeply, tasting her essence on the air. "You don't have to." His cock reared up against his stomach, and the muscles in his thighs tightened.

"What are you? Some kind of magician?"

"No. It's not a trick. I'm nude. I couldn't hide wires."

"That's too weird."

He watched as curiosity displaced her libido. That couldn't be allowed. "I have more to show you."

"Really?" She looked expectantly at him.

Gently he pushed her back, one knee between her thighs, the other straddling her hips, as he kissed her. His tongue delved deep inside, thrusting, mating with hers in frenzy. She moaned into his mouth and ground her hips into his knee, and he groaned with need for her.

This was his woman. She would be his. Always.

His hand found her breast, and he kneaded the soft flesh then teased the nipple with soft swirls over the silky-skinned peak. His cock was rock hard, his balls achy and tight. It took every bit of his willpower to resist plunging deep inside. It wasn't time. Yet.

He shifted his weight and moved his knee to the outside of her hips. Then he concentrated on her taste as he licked and nipped her neck, shoulders and breasts. She arched her back, lifting her tits high in the air, and he gave each one the attention it deserved. With one hand pinching and teasing one nipple, he rimmed the other with his tongue and blew on the wetness. The pink skin puckered, the erect nub hard and ripe.

The hunger coursing through his being was almost overwhelming, so intense he trembled. Yet he forced himself to go slow. Next, would be her stomach, which he explored with hands and tongue before arriving at the thatch of curly hair below.

Muscles tense, heart thumping, mouth dry, he lifted her knees, parted her legs wide and drunk in the sight of her. Damn, what an amazing sight! Her soft, feminine body open to him, her cunt lips swollen, pink, and dripping wet. He smelled her juices, heard her quick breathing, tasted her skin in his mouth. The assault on his every sense was mind-blowing.

He dropped his head and inhaled, relishing the musky scent of her, and parted her lips with his fingers. She stretched her legs wider, silently welcoming his exploration. He started with a fingertip, rimming her outer lips in slow, wide circles. When her breath caught, he slipped it between her folds, sliding in her sweet juices until he found the tight bud lying in wait.

With his first touch, her thigh muscles tensed, pulling her legs even wider apart. With his first lick, her stomach tightened, lifting her mound to his face.

He was on the verge of losing control. Her body was so ripe, so ready for him, and his cock was so damn hard it hurt. Still, he wouldn't fuck her. Not yet.

Instead, he flicked his tongue over her clit until she shuddered with need, then slid two fingers into her sodden pussy, pumping in and out until she cried for more.

"Please, please fuck me now."

Her willful submission drove him mad with need, yet he refused to give in…until she rolled over onto her stomach and lifted her ass into the air.

Soft flesh begging for his touch sat inches from his face. He parted her luscious cheeks, tasted her ass, and slid his fingers into her tight pussy. She rocked back and forth on her hands and knees, driving his fingers deeper.

Then he slipped those delving fingers out of her pussy and pressed on her tight hole, and she opened to him with a sigh.

* * * * *

Jane was going crazy. Stark raving mad, thanks to Josh. What did he do to her body! What was he doing to her mind, and her heart? Holy shit! It had to be against the law.

She concentrated on relaxing her ass muscles, welcoming his finger inside, but the moment he broke the barrier, she felt herself hurling toward climax.

She couldn't come yet! He hadn't even gotten inside yet! She had to have him inside.

"Stop!" she pleaded.

He slid his finger out, and her asshole closed tight again. Her pussy muscles clenched then relaxed, so close to the spasm of an orgasm she could feel it in her throat.

"What's wrong?"

"You. I mean…" She sat facing him. "I want you inside of me. What do I have to do to get it? You're driving me crazy." Shit, looking at his flushed face and rumpled hair was enough to send her over the edge, and those arms...and that chest...and that cock!

"Show me how much you need me."

"Haven't I done that already?" She sat back and brazenly parted her legs. "Look at me! I'm sopping wet."

Oh, that was a hot expression. "Show me more," he grumbled.

She ran her hands over her tits, then down her stomach to her mound. "Look at my pussy, swollen and ready for you. So tight." The folds were slick as she ran her finger down the center. She parted the inner lips and slid a finger inside, concentrating on clamping the inner muscles around her finger. That felt damn good!

"Oh, yeah." He smiled a lopsided grin. "And your ass. I love your ass."

She turned around and lifted it up to his face. "Look at my ass. Do you want to fuck it?"

"Oh, yeah. I'll make it so good for you."

Swallowing a lump of fear, having never been fucked in the ass, but assuming it hurt like hell, she swayed her hips in front of him. "Fuck it. I want you to."

"Are you sure? I promise I'll go slow. Do you trust me?"

"I trust you."

He growled and left, returning a moment later with a tube of lubricant and a condom.

What had she just gotten herself into? She watched as he opened the tube, never more conscious of his huge girth.

"Give me your hand, love." He handed her the condom, and she slid it on him.

Holding out her hand to him again, he squeezed onto her palm a large blob of the slick goop then he motioned toward his cock. Her gaze locked to his, she wrapped her hand around his thick cock and squeezed. His eyelids fell closed and his expression turned hard. That was encouraging. She liked to see him taking pleasure as well as giving it. She slowly slid her hand down to the base and then back up to the head several times, feeling the twitch of muscle lying under the velvety skin through the condom cover. "How's that?"

"Good. Now let me have that ass."

She kneeled on all fours and braced herself for pain. The probing of his cock's head between her parted ass cheeks sent waves of heat to her pussy. Her gut clenched, her face flamed, and her breathing rasped in her own ears. She concentrated on opening to him, relaxing her muscles. She inhaled slowly and exhaled, wanting to resist the probing of his cock, yet also wanting to feel it inside.

Then that impossibly huge head broke the barrier and her ass muscle, which felt stretched beyond belief, clamped tight around it.

"Oh my God!" She'd never felt anything like this. It was…beyond words. Beyond comprehension. This was the ultimate test of trust. The ultimate giving. The ultimate pleasure.

Heat rocketed through her body as he pushed that glorious cock deeper into her ass. Her mind shut off completely, and only the rawest of sensations reached her. The sound of his groans of pleasure, the feel of his fingers digging into her ass cheeks, the pounding of her own heart in her ribcage. The breath that had caught somewhere between her lungs and her mouth.

She was going to come. Just like that. She felt the orgasm begin in the pit of her stomach and spread outward, and just as he sunk himself to the hilt into her ass, her pussy and ass spasmed in a body-wracking orgasm.

She gasped and rode wave after wave of orgasm as her ass milked Josh's swollen cock. The sweet pulsing seemed to last an eternity, and she prayed it would never end. Yet, eventually it did. As the last twitches exploded through her body, he slipped out.

Suddenly she felt very empty. Her head cleared, and her speaking function returned. "How the hell do you do that?" she asked between panting breaths.

"Do what?"

"Hold out?"

"It's all in the head. Delaying orgasm only makes the lovemaking all that much more enjoyable. It's not all about getting the big-O. It's about giving pleasure. It's about loving your body, soul and spirit."

"All well and good, but I couldn't hold out."

"That's good. I want you to lose control. But I hope you're good for another round because I'm not through with you yet." He winked.

Much to her surprise, she found herself hot with need all over again.

"This time, I'm on top." He forced her onto her back, and she didn't resist, enjoying the way his firm touch felt. There was something thrilling about his taking charge in lovemaking. She loved it. He slid off the condom, parted her legs and stroked her clit. "Such a beautiful pussy. Such a beautiful, loving, giving woman."

She felt her thighs and stomach tighten as he forced her legs wider. Then he kneeled between them, his body at a ninety-degree angle to hers, and plunged deep inside.

"Oh God!" She opened herself wider, wishing his cock would touch her deepest parts. She felt so alive. So whole. So loved. She opened her eyes and looked up, shocked to see him relaxed and smiling down at her. Tender love was etched in his every feature, from his sparkling eyes to his broad smile. Even though he wasn't speaking the words, she knew, she heard them with her heart.

She wanted to be his forever. She wanted to have his children, to celebrate his joys and hold him in sorrow. He was her future. She didn't want to think of living another day without him.

*I love you, Josh. Forever.*

She reached up and intertwined her fingers with his, squeezing his hands, and he squeezed back, sending a steady current of electricity into her palms. Warmth buzzed up her arms, over her chest, and down her stomach. It tickled her insides, hopping around in the pit of her belly before shooting south and settling between her legs. She sighed.

The zaps increased in frequency, and instead of tickling warmth, smoldering heat flamed through her body. He steadily loved her, his cock sliding out, hovering just outside her weeping pussy then plunging deep inside. He released one of her hands, and pinched her clit. White bolts played before her eyes, and her body stiffened. She gasped in surprise and joy, overwhelmed by the sensations and emotions roiling inside her like a tempest.

Her pussy clamped onto him, pulling him deeper, willing him to never leave. Suddenly she rocketed toward another orgasm, completely unable to stop herself. Every muscle in her body tensed, even cramping the soles of her feet.

"Slow, love." He stopped moving inside and lifted his fingers from her clit. "Don't come yet. We'll come together."

"Oh…" He wasn't asking for much! Having him inside at last was making her insane, and he wanted her to wait for him? She tried to hold back, taking inventory of each sensation, hoping that might slow her eager body to meet his pace. She relaxed her muscles, beginning with the ones clamped tight around his cock.

"That's it." He pumped in and out, slowly at first, then gaining speed. He reached down and found her clit again, and she bit back a yelp.

She was in agony, sheer, sweet agony. His cock was slamming into her pussy, his finger tracing circles over her clit, her soul soaring to the heavens.

"Now! Come now for me."

She drew in a deep breath and willed herself to go over the edge, and just as she heard him growl with his own release, she found hers.

Together, they rode the waves of pulsing, throbbing release until they dropped from exhaustion.

# Chapter Thirteen

*Great sex works better than any truth serum.*

"I think I'm dead." Spread eagle next to Josh, Jane struggled to catch her breath. Every part of her body was weak as could be, like warm gelatin. She figured she wouldn't be able to move for at least a couple of days. But as the glow of climax cooled, and her mind began functioning again, she found herself surprised by her own behavior. Had she really let him fuck her in the ass? "I can't believe it."

"Can't believe what?"

"What I've done with you. I've never done those things with another person before. I've never wanted to."

"Good." He raised himself up on an elbow and rested an index finger under her chin. "And you will never do them with anyone else."

Those words were like food for the soul. The Halleluiah Chorus echoed through her head. "So, you're serious about this marriage stuff?" *Hal-le-lu-ia!*

"Dead serious. Why?"

"I don't know. Men say lots of things in the throes of passion. Make promises they don't mean. Make demands they don't really want. I guess I thought you might be goofing around. Playing."

His smile was playful, but reassuring. "I might like to play, but not about something like marriage. I'm serious. What about you?"

*Yes! But I'm scared. Tell him! This is important.* "I don't know. I mean. I..." Oh God, she hated saying these words the first time. "I think...no, I know I'm...falling in love with you." *Yikes! I said it!* "But it's so soon. We barely know each other."

"I know I love you. I've told you that already."

*And you'd better not ever stop!* "How can you know that for certain? What if I'm a nutcase?"

"I know you're a nutcase, and I still love you." He kissed her nose, and she smiled, giggles bubbling in her stomach.

She traced the line between his pecs, following it down the center of his stomach. It was such a sexy line. "Well, what if I was really crazy, like an ax murderer?"

"You're not."

"Or a child molester."

"You're not that, either."

"Can I ask you a question, then?" She drew a circle around his belly button. That was one cute belly button!

"Sure!"

"What is it about me?" She glanced up at his face.

He huddled his brows together. "What do you mean?"

Deciding she was too nervous to look him in the eye, she returned her gaze to his belly. "I mean you're rich—like Donald Trump loaded—and drop-dead gorgeous. You could have anyone you wanted, movie stars, models. Why settle for me? I'm just a plain-Jane. A nobody."

He slid his arm under her head and wrapped his other arm around her waist, pulling her tightly against him. The heat emanating from his body nearly stung it was so intense. The genuine love and warmth of his embrace made her want to stay there forever. "First, you are not a nobody."

"Well, you know what I mean. I'm not famous."

"I don't care about that."

"And I'm not beautiful—"

"Yes, you are." He slipped a fingertip under her chin and lifted it until she met his gaze. "You are the most beautiful woman in the world to me."

She didn't know whether to laugh or cry. In all her years, no one had ever said those words to her. Not Greg. Not anyone. "But I'm overweight—"

"Not in my eyes. Your body is beautiful, soft in all the right places. Strong. Sexy."

"I'm nothing special."

"Yes, you are." He palmed her cheek, and she let her head rest in his hand. His thumb brushed her cheek. "There are so many reasons to love you, Jane. No man in his right mind could avoid falling in love with you. You're smart. Funny. Adventurous. Giving. Loving. Trusting." He smiled. "Do you need me to continue?"

"By all means! I've never had anyone describe me that way. Wow, I feel like a queen! Keep them coming! Or did you run out of compliments already?"

"I could go on forever. In my eyes you are a queen."

Her heart melted. *This man is too wonderful for words.* "You're definitely prime king material, too." Thankful for the moment this man walked into her life, she wrapped her arms around him and squeezed. "King of my heart." She smiled. "I have another question. How do you know so much about me? From the get-go you knew what car I drove, where I lived. Did you run a background check? I don't blame you if you did."

"No, I didn't. You can blame a friend of yours."

She tried to sit up, but he held her down. "Diana?"

He nodded. "Yep."

"I knew it!" She broke loose from his embrace and sitting, slapped her thigh. "That little schemer. What else did she tell you?"

"I won't tell."

"Oh yeah?" She leaned over him, her hands pressed palm down on the floor on either side of his shoulders. She bent low until her face was inches from his. "You'd better."

He smiled. "Or what?"

She pressed her nose against his. "You'll be sorry."

"Oh. Well, I wouldn't want to be that. I give, but I won't be specific. Let's just put it this way, I know more about you than you think."

"Well, that's no fair!" She sat back and crossed her arms over her chest. "I don't know squat about you."

"What do you want to know?"

"Where you came from, your roots, your dreams and ambitions, your fears."

"Okay. Well, I told you where I grew up. I have thirteen brothers and sisters—"

The air shot from her lungs. "Thirteen? As in one more than twelve? Holy shit!"

"Large families are pretty normal in our community."

"Your poor mother!"

"Outside of the fact that she was pregnant for almost fifteen years straight, she had it good. My father was a good provider, although we didn't see him much until we were older."

"That's not my idea of good. I don't want to be pregnant for fifteen years. And I don't want a husband who's gone all the time."

He smiled. "I'm glad you feel that way—about the husband part, at least." He rolled onto his back and folded his arms under his head. "Now, for the other things you wanted to know. Let me see. My dreams are to marry you, fuck you silly, and have a brood of kids."

*Oh, shit!* "Then you weren't joking about that either?"

"Nope."

"Oh." She dropped her hand to her stomach, wondering what it might feel like to have a child in there.

"You'll be a wonderful mother."

"I don't know if I'm ready. The idea of being a mother scares me silly."

"Don't worry. When the time comes, you'll be ready. So, that covers my roots and my dreams. What else was there? Oh, yeah. My ambitions. I am to be king one day soon—"

"King? Of Canada? Aren't they ruled by England's queen?"

"No! I mean…king of my family." He sat up and ran his fingers through his hair, sending the silky curls in disarray. "Head honcho. Ruler. Isn't the husband supposed to be king of his household?"

"I can see you have a thing about power," she teased.

"Not exactly."

"King? Come on! I mean, I know what I said earlier, but I was being silly. You don't really expect your little wifey to be barefoot, pregnant and waiting on you hand and foot all day, do you?"

He grinned and shook his head. "That sounds nice."

She reached for the nearest thing she could find, the blanket he'd so lovingly wrapped her in earlier, and clubbed him with it.

"Hey! What was that for?"

"For all the crimes you've committed against independent women around the world."

"Believe me, I've committed no crimes. My wife will be treated so well, and have so much, she'll be thrilled to serve me."

After a quick assessing gaze of the room they were in, Jane could almost believe that. Still the whole serve-the-man thing rankled her nerves. "What about your fears? Obviously you know mine."

"My worst fear is of losing you."

"Give me a—"

He swept her into his arms and held her tight. "I mean it. I don't ever want to live a day without you."

By God, the man meant what he was saying. There was no way to fake that genuine expression. She couldn't speak.

"I love you. I will take care of you, protect you. You'll have the best the world has to offer, travel, fine jewels, a beautiful home, children, whatever you desire. You will be treated like a queen."

"It's not all about what I get out of the deal, you know."

"I'll cherish you. There's no man alive that'll treat you as good as I will."

This whole thing sounded like a dream…that, or a line out of a Lifetime movie that ends up with the guy being an obsessive psychopath, hell-bent on destroying the poor woman. How would she determine which it was? She knew what she wanted to believe.

"Trust yourself to know the difference."

See? Like that stuff! What did he do? Have some kind of wire installed in her brain so he could hear her thoughts? She'd ignored that for long enough. "How the hell do you do that? You're reading my mind."

"No one can read your mind. I'm just guessing, like I said before."

"No way."

"We're in tune, connected. Mind, body and spirit. We're meant to be together." He slid his hand down between her legs, and her pussy thrummed. He pulled her knees apart, and her face heated. He parted her lips and teased her clit with a fluttering tongue.

Her whole body lit aflame. Damn, he was good at that!

He slipped a finger inside, hooking it to rub against the sensitive upper wall. That just about did it for her. She was lost. She had to have him. Again.

Then, he stopped.

She was left a panting, throbbing, sopping mass of need. She gasped. "What's wrong?"

"Nothing."

"Then why did you stop?"

"Oh, I don't know. I thought maybe you were tired."

"Not too tired."

He smiled and laid back. "Show me."

She obliged, enjoying the change in position, first, kneeling and taking him into her mouth. He tasted of man and woman, sex and sweetness. He smelled masculine, musky but good at the same time, and his moans of pleasure did things only tongues would normally do to her pussy.

Wanting to show him pleasure like he'd never had, she opened her mouth wide and slid down, down, down his cock, taking each tasty inch into her mouth until her nose was at the base. Then she cupped his balls in her hand and teased them.

"Damn, woman! Shit!"

She slid up and down his length several more times, fingers exploring every minute detail of his balls and ass, and then, wetting her finger in her mouth, she plunged it into his ass and his rock-hard thigh muscles tensed into tight ribbons.

"Fuck me," he gasped.

Enjoying the feeling of control, she sat up, smiled into his flushed face and straddled his cock. Then she sat, slowly, allowing the tip to merely press against her pussy. She rotated her hips, grinding her folds against him until she was so ready she couldn't wait another minute and she sank down.

Oh…

She raised herself up and slammed back down again, watching Josh's scorching expression as he watched her body work. His gaze strayed from her face to her tits then down to their joining before winding back up to her face.

"This is what making love is all about." He held out his palms. "Hold my hands."

She took his hands in hers, and felt the electric charge zap through her body again, kick-starting her heart, stealing her breath, and rocketing to her pussy where it ignited an explosion so powerful she practically fell over. She dropped forward against Josh's chest, and more electricity surged through her body until every muscle was convulsing. Josh rolled her onto her back and rammed that cock deep and hard, over and over.

"Oh God!" Those mind-melting contractions wouldn't end. They just kept going, and going, and going.

Then Josh sucked in a deep breath, blasted out a cry and stiffened, sending his cum deep inside.

As she struggled to catch her breath, snuggled safe and warm against Josh's chest, she uttered three words, "I love you."

Would she really have to leave this place and return to her life? Or could she just stay there forever?

*****

The next day—Monday, ugh!—was so normal, Jane almost went crazy with boredom, at least until lunch. Then, true to form, Diana got in Jane's face and things got ugly.

"You've got to be kidding me." Diana slammed her fist on the table. "You aren't marrying him so soon! I love you, but are you insane?"

"I'm not kidding."

Diana reached out and knocked on Jane's skull. "Hello? Is anyone home?"

"My mental capacity is firmly in place." Jane dumped a blob of ketchup on her plate and tried to act like her friend's sarcasm wasn't hurting.

"Damn. I was hoping this change was temporary. I hate to be the one to tell you this, but you've lost it, sweetie."

"Maybe you're just jealous." Jane's stomach was tied in knots she hated confrontation so much, but she tried to eat. She popped a French fry into her mouth and washed it down with a swig of soda.

"Jealous? Me? Not a chance."

"You said yourself he wouldn't give you the time of day. Remember? You know, I understand if you're jealous. I think I would be if things were reversed."

"If it had bothered me, I'd never have introduced you to him. I wouldn't have told him all about you, either. I practically gave him your social security number. Don't get me wrong. I don't want to tell you who you can and cannot date, but I'm worried about you. You've changed. I thought you might date for a while, take things safe and slow like the Jane I used to know and love."

"Well, maybe that Jane is gone."

"I don't know if I like this Jane. She's pretty damn crazy. Then again, crazy isn't all bad."

"And you're not?" Jane smiled, trying to ease the tension. She took a sip of cola and tried to sort out the thoughts racing through her mind. "Please, try to understand. I didn't expect you to jump with joy—not that I wouldn't have appreciated that—but I was hoping for quiet acceptance. I'm happier than I've ever been. I can't stop thinking about him. I want to be with him. All the time."

Diana resumed eating, taking a dainty bite of her burger. That was a good sign. At least she'd chilled out enough to eat. "I can understand that. What if he's not what you think, though?"

"I don't believe he's anything but what I've seen."

"Not all people are honest, you know."

"I know that. I'm not a baby."

"Well, you're not exactly acting like a responsible adult right now—"

Jane shoved the rest of her lunch into the bag and shook her head. "You're being mean, and I don't need to sit here and take that. I can get that back at the office from asshole." She stood and reached for her glass.

Diana caught her wrist. "Sorry. Please, stay. I'm just worried about you. Can't a friend worry?"

Jane sat. "Yes. But do you have to be such a ball buster all the time? Try to understand where I'm coming from."

"I think I understand more than you do. That's why I'm having such a problem with this. I'm not trying to be mean. Your divorce was final only weeks ago, and now you're jumping into another marriage."

When put that way, it did sound alarming.

Diana continued. "I think you're grieving and lonely and jumping at the first opportunity to regain what you think you've lost."

*That makes sense, but it's not true. How can I make her see that?* "I might be lonely, but I think I'm way past the grief part."

"What's wrong with just slowing things down a little? Maybe a lengthy engagement?"

"Listen." Jane leveled her gaze at Diana's worried face. "I'm fine. I'm over what's-his-name. Way over. I've found the most amazing man I've ever met. We fit together in every way. I never felt that way about Greg, even when things were good. I just know this is right. Try to be happy for me. Please."

"I can't. Not yet. Marrying him this early will be a mistake."

Jane stood and shook her head. "I'm sorry then. I was hoping you'd be more supportive, maybe even agree to be my maid of honor. I guess I'll ask Carmen instead."

"She won't either."

"Let her tell me that for herself then, and quit being such a pushy, manipulative bitch." Jane shoved the door open and charged out to the parking lot.

Diana followed her, catching her arm. Her eyes wet with tears. Her lips trembled. "Please. I'm sorry. I'm doing it because I love you." She cried, her sniffles and quiet sobs soothing Jane's anger. "Someday, when you're left pregnant and penniless and big restaurateur—or whatever the hell he is—Josh has dumped you for a younger bimbo, you'll see that. Just like you did last time."

"I appreciate your worry, but that was different. Greg was an ass right from the start. Josh would never do what Greg did."

"Don't ever say never."

"Josh didn't go for you, did he?"

Diana's eyes widened and she released Jane's arms. "What's that supposed to mean?"

"I know Greg was hot on your ass from day one."

"He was not!"

"Whatever." Jane opened her car door and sat. "Come on, or we'll be late."

"I can't believe you just inferred I was after Greg. You know what I think of that rat."

"I was not inferring anything. I was just pointing out that he likes your type. I have no idea why that man married me. Then, compare Greg to Josh. Josh isn't attracted to you, not that I can understand it since every man I know thinks you're hot. But I appreciate it because that means he won't stray. Get my logic?"

"That is some of the most convoluted logic I've ever heard…outside of my own." Diana sat in the passenger seat and closed the door. "So, when's the wedding?"

"Does that mean you'll be my maid of honor?"

"I guess." Diana smiled. "I can't let my best friend down, even if I think she's making a big…huge…colossal… mistake."

Jane ignored the jitters parading down her spine. "That's left to be seen." She drove back to the office, gave Diana a quick wave, and headed back to her cubicle, stacked high with work she simply hadn't been able to concentrate on earlier.

And that wasn't any easier now, either.

Although Jane's mind was busy hopping back and forth between her work and Josh, time dragged by at a slug's jogging pace. Finally, the five o'clock hour lumbered by, and she cleaned her desk and shut off her computer.

# Chapter Fourteen

*Food and sex naturally fit together, like sand and surf or birthdays and chocolate cake.*

Josh stood on her front porch, a giant cooler that could practically fit a dead cow sat at his feet. A naughty smile spread over his face.

Oh boy! She parked the car and half-ran, half-skipped up the walkway. "Hi."

"Hi." He gazed down at her with eyes that shone with hunger. "I brought dinner."

"Oh." No wonder she saw hunger. She unlocked the front door and held it open for him as he hefted the giant cooler into her living room.

Then, just as she was about to let it fall closed, he caught it. "I have a few more things outside." He looked like a kid on Christmas, giddy and playful.

"Okay." She alternately glanced at the cooler and back outside. What was he up to?

He carried in a duffel bag and dropped it next to the cooler. "Okay. Are you hungry?"

"Starved."

"Good! Strip."

"Strip what?"

There was that wicked grin again. "Yourself."

"I have to eat naked?"

He wrinkled his nose. "Eating off of clothing isn't very pleasant."

"What?"

"You get lint in your food."

"You're making no sense."

"Trust me and take off your clothes."

"Okay." She slowly shed her clothes, beginning with her jacket, and not for a single fraction of a moment was she unaware of his increasingly hot gaze on her. It was like a laser beam, heating her skin wherever it traveled, down her throat, over her breasts, down her stomach and between her legs.

Her knees were a little wobbly.

"You are absolutely stunning. Perfect."

She felt her cheeks flame. "Your turn."

His gaze riveted to her face, he shed his shirt, exposing those amazing abs and arms—yum! That sight alone was enough to stir her appetite. Then he slid off his shoes and socks and worked his pants down his legs. A pair of black athletic boxers hugged his balls and erection, and she felt her pussy practically drip with need.

Off came the shorts, and she was face to face with a fully nude Josh, a man who possessed the world's most perfect body.

"Now, we eat."

She could think of a million other things she'd like to do first. "Okay."

He rummaged through the duffel bag and pulled out a big blue thing. Plastic? What? He moved the coffee table and side chairs, creating a large open area in the middle of the living room, then unfolded the large plastic tablecloth, nearly the size of a single bedspread, and laid it on the floor. "Don't want to ruin your nice floor."

Ruin?

Next he opened the cooler, and she listened to clinking and clunking. He pulled out a bottle of wine and sat, leaning casually against the couch base. With a pat on the floor, he welcomed her to sit next to him.

"Where are the glasses?"

"We don't need them."

How else was there to drink wine? Out of the bottle like a bum? Well, she wasn't too good to do that, she supposed.

"Lie down."

That wasn't what she'd expected. Was he going to pour it down her throat? She'd choke for sure! "I'm not much into drinking games—"

"Trust me. Just lie down. I won't hurt you."

Her body tingled with anticipation as she lay down. What was he going to do?

On his knees, he scooted around to her side then held the bottle over her stomach and poured a small puddle onto her belly. He grinned, and she giggled, making the wine spill over her side and trickle down to the floor.

He pouted. "You spilled my wine."

She bit her lip, trying not to laugh. "Sorry."

He gave an exaggerated sigh and poured more. "Now hold still." Then he leaned down and licked the wine off her skin.

Wow! What a feeling, his tongue laving her stomach, dipping suggestively into her belly button. She felt her nerves come alive, impulses jumping and charging through her body. She bent her legs and tipped her pelvis up as he worked his way down.

When he kissed her, the flavor of the wine, melded with the taste of her skin and him shot flaming cannonballs to her pussy. His kiss was slow, dipping and delving into every region of her mouth. His soft lips worked in unison with his tongue in a kiss that was quickly draining her lungs and brain.

She needed his touch. Between her legs.

He sat up, smiled, and held up the bottle. "Would you care for some? It's rude to drink alone."

She couldn't imagine wine tasting better than off that man's body. "Sure. I'm game!" She waited for him to lie down, then poured a small puddle onto his stomach. Unlike on her, it ran in streams between his developed stomach muscles, not that it mattered. Merely a taste was all she wanted.

What a taste she got! Who would have thought wine could taste so good. She felt a warm buzz spread through her body, carried away from her stomach in pleasant waves. "Yum."

She straddled him, her pussy wet and ready and rubbed it up and down his erection. He caught her hips, holding them hostage and not allowing her to slide down that glorious cock.

"Not yet, love. We still have to eat."

Eat? Like hell! She was ready to fuck.

He gently set her on the mat and sat up. "I'm glad you're so receptive, but it's more fun to make yourself wait."

"Maybe for you. I'm impatient."

He laughed and pulled out a small container of something. "Lie on your stomach."

She did as he asked, resting her head on her crossed arms, and felt something warm and smooth dripping on her back and ass. In reflex, her lower back muscles tensed, arching her spine and thrusting her ass higher.

"Oh, nice. I love your ass, so soft and smooth." He parted her cheeks and she felt more warm liquid run down her crack and drip from her pussy. Then he proceeded to lick every drop away.

Oh, this was torture! Wonderful, aching, pulsing torture, and she was loving every minute of it.

When he finished laving her ass cheeks, he parted them and worked the same magic to her crack, his tongue flickering and delving lower and lower. She arched her back, willing him to find his way to her sodden pussy, but he stopped just short of it.

"Turn over."

*Anything you say, sexy.* No way she'd complain about that command. Over she went, appreciating the sight of his encouraging smile as she rested back. Once she'd made herself comfortable, he tipped the container over her chest, pouring a stream of the liquid over first one nipple and then the other.

Licking, suckling, at each nipple, he brought her body to muscle clenching, eyelid scrunching need. Her stomach gripped into a tight ball and she lifted her knees. Finally he worked his way down, down, down, easing her knees apart to open her pussy to him.

The first touch of his tongue nearly did her in, but she fought the urge to give herself over to the climax. She wanted him inside, filling her, fucking her mindless, when she came.

Resisting wasn't easy when the man's tongue was drawing slow, luscious circles over her clit. Just the right tempo, just the right pressure. Oh... She was losing the battle.

Her foot muscles went into spasm and as if he knew, he massaged each one, his mouth still hungrily lapping, drinking her juices. He pushed her thighs wider, her knees out to the sides, making her clit even more sensitive to his every touch, and she felt a steady growing ball of warmth in her gut. It wouldn't be long...

He stopped.

Dizzy with need, she opened her eyes.

"Are you hungry?" he asked.

"No."

"Thirsty?"

"No."

"You make a wonderful plate."

"This plate needs a good reaming."

"I can accommodate that. If..."

"Oh, for God's sake! I'll beg. I'll do whatever you want."

"I'll fuck you if you'll eat one bite first." He plucked up something from the container he'd been pouring from and held it to her mouth.

Not caring what it was, she took it. Salty. Fishy? She swallowed. Not what she'd expected at all. It wasn't half bad. "What was that?"

"Tuna steak."

"Tuna? You're sick! Whatever happened to whipped cream? Or cherries? Or chocolate syrup? Tuna as a love toy? Only you'd come up with something so—"

He drove his cock to the hilt into her pussy and all thought ceased. Her pussy stretched around him then clamped tight, and she moaned. His cock fit perfectly, filling her to the brim, tickling that spot at the top that sent wave upon wave of juices over him.

He pulled out until the tip teased her lips and then plunged deep inside again. She welcomed him, consciously closing her pussy around him, and enjoyed the increasing flush spreading out from their juncture.

"I love the way you do that. You're so tight. So wet." He slid in and out, slowly, letting her feel each inch as it escaped and then filled her.

She sighed, lifted her arms to loop them around his neck and kissed him. It was a slow, lazy kiss that matched the pace of their lovemaking. His tongue slipped into her mouth where it stroked hers. Sensual, it left her feeling warm from head to toe. Then he withdrew it, and her tongue followed his, into his mouth. He sucked, drawing it deeper and deeper as his cock probed her pussy.

Then, with no warning, he broke the kiss, pulled his cock from her, and dove for the duffle bag sitting just out of arm's reach on the floor.

"I have a surprise for you."

"What kind of surprise?" Frustrated but also curious, she pushed herself up, watching him rummage through the bag.

"It's not much. I wanted to see if you like it. Lie back and close your eyes."

"Okay." Dying to know what he was up to, she dropped onto her back again and lifted her knees, drawing them together. She heard a snap, like the sound of a lotion bottle's lid popping open. Then she felt Josh putting pressure on her knees, pushing them back and out. "Just tell me you aren't into torture."

"Of course not. Only pleasure, love. Trust me. This will be wonderful."

"I do." Her body tensed as she waited. She felt the softest touch to her pussy as he parted her labia and touched her clit, making tiny, slow circles over it.

Gradually, a flush of heat settled over her clit, making it super-sensitive. Every touch intensified, driving her instantly crazy. She loved it. She hated it.

"Oh!" She gripped whatever she could in her fists and held on, raking her fingernails through the carpet. "Oh my God!"

"Do you like it?"

She gasped, pulling her legs wider apart, and wishing he'd plunge that glorious cock of his deep inside. Her pussy was empty. Miserably, achingly empty. "What is it? It's such a strange feeling."

"Does it hurt?"

"No..."

"Do you want me to continue?"

Her lungs were losing air, and she struggled to re-inflate them. Her pussy was practically on fire, and yet she couldn't resist begging for more. Her body was tense from hair follicle to toe. "More! Oh, please!"

"I have another surprise. Would you like me to get it?"

"Yes!"

Her body instantly relaxed when he lifted his fingertip from her clit, but the brief relief wasn't nearly long enough. The real torture began.

A soft buzzing vibration rimmed her pussy. The vibrator was almost silent, yet she heard the buzz inside her head as it meandered around her pussy while avoiding directly touching it. In reflex, she tipped her hips, silently willing Josh to thrust it inside, to fill the void within.

"This is torture. I thought you said you weren't into torture."

"It may be, but it isn't pain, love."

"That's up for debate."

He chuckled. "What do you want? Tell me."

"I want you to fuck me."

He clucked his tongue. "You are mighty impatient."

"I never claimed to be patient. Now, do something about it! Or I'll take matters into my own hands."

"As much as I'd adore watching that, I'm not going to let you. Lie back. Enjoy. I'm serving you."

"You're killing me, not serving me."

He chuckled again. "Exactly what I was hoping for."

She opened her eyes and watched as he dipped his head down and, his gaze riveted to hers, he teased her nipple, circling it with his tongue and then nibbling. The vibrator wandered up over her mound and stomach before stopping over the other nipple.

Her back reflexively arched, pushing her breasts up. Oh, what that bizarre-looking thing did to her body! And the man wielding it! Her eyelids, too heavy to remain open, fell closed, and she sighed.

"I want you to know the ultimate pleasure. Will you explore with me?"

Ultimate pleasure? Did it get any better than this? "Explore?"

"Yes. Let me show you what you've been missing." He dragged the vibrator back down her stomach and teased her labia with it.

She tensed, hoping he'd push it into her pussy. Her breaths came in gasps. Her heart drummed in her head. Her hands clenched and unclenched around themselves. "You have. Oh…"

"This is only the beginning. There are so many things you haven't seen yet," he whispered into her ear. His breath tickled her neck, sending a flood of goosebumps down the right side of her body.

Hot and cold. Pleasure and need. She was a bundle of contradicting sensations. And she couldn't make sense of anything.

He was speaking, making promises, yet she could no more understand his words than if he were speaking Greek. His voice wandered around in her head, drifting like a breeze. His touches ignited her skin. His smell filled her nostrils, and she drew in as deep a breath as she could, adoring the scent.

"Turn over," she heard him say, and she rolled over.

"On your hands and knees, love."

She pushed herself up on arms so wobbly they collapsed under her weight. She opened her eyes but immediately shut them again. The world was dipping and spinning like a carnival ride.

Did she take some kind of drug?

"It's all right. Your body isn't used to so much stimulation. This way." He helped her crawl across the living room and settle her chest on the couch. She folded her arms and rested her head on top of them. "I want to make you feel like you've never felt before. Would you like that?"

"Yes."

Inch by inch, he pushed his cock into her sodden pussy. When it was buried deep, pressing against the most sensitive parts inside her, he groaned.

Her body flamed.

"Damn, you make this hard."

*And you don't?* She tried to speak, but couldn't. Instead, she rocked back a little, taking a fraction of an inch more of him inside.

One hand kneaded her ass as he pulled his cock out and then thrust back inside again.

Her breath left her body in a huff. Then the vibrator appeared again, slipping between her ass cheeks and pushing at her hole.

*Oh my God! Oh my God!"* The zapping vibrations hummed through her pussy and ass, igniting nerves everywhere. She felt herself burning up.

"Open yourself to me. Take all the pleasure I have to give." He pulled his cock out then pushed the vibrator into her ass as he pushed his cock into her pussy. She willed her ass to take it inside.

The tip eased inside her ass as his cock plunged into her pussy. Her body clenched, hurling toward orgasm with such speed and intensity, she couldn't breathe.

More of the vibrator hummed inside, filling her more, and more, and more as his cock slammed in and out twice. Oh, she was going insane! As she climbed toward the summit, all sensations blended. She tasted smells, saw sounds, heard touches. Her thoughts became sparks of light in a field of darkness. They swirled around and around as her spirit soared to the stars.

There, at her side, was Josh, his skin translucent, his heart beating in the center of his chest. A smile of love upon his lips.

"I will love you for all eternity," his promise echoed through time and space.

# Chapter Fifteen

*When your gut instinct smacks you upside the head, it's time to listen.*

After three long, tiring days, and two wonderful nights spent with Josh, Jane was ready for the weekend, already. Thanks to Carmen's work schedule, being a nurse on swing shift, their girl's night out was Thursday for the next four weeks. Lucky for Jane, tonight Diana was determined to get into that nightclub, come hell or high water.

Yippee.

Hoping to find an excuse to duck out of the whole thing, Jane used Diana's phone to check her messages. One new message. Jane's heart skipped a beat. Josh's voice buzzed in her ear then spread through her body, like only Josh's voice did. "Hi, love. I have to see you tonight. I know you have plans, and I swear I'm not trying to ruin them for you. I can't go on like this. Not another moment. I must see you. Please come to my place? Tonight?"

Now, that sounded important. Much too important to ignore. Ladies' Night at the Wolf Den would have to wait. *Gee, too bad.* She grabbed her purse and knocked on Diana's bathroom door. "Diana, I have to go."

The door flew open, revealing Diana's face, covered with green slime and her hair wound around rollers the size of Josh's forearm. "What are you talking about? Have to go where?"

"It's important."

"What?"

"Something personal."

"It's him, isn't it?"

"Maybe."

"Damn it!" Diana slammed her fist into the doorframe. "He won't give you any room to breathe. Can't you see that? He's taking over every aspect of your life, won't even let you go out with us. He's a control freak."

"He is not, and he apologized for ruining my plans. He said it's important. It can't wait."

"You're in way too deep here." Diana gripped Jane's arms and gave her a stern, intimidating—or at least Jane assumed it was meant to be intimidating—stare. It wasn't easy taking Diana seriously looking like that. Green goo had a way of stealing some of the intimidation factor. "I love you. I can't stand seeing you like this, bowing to his every command. You're his little puppet."

"Hey, I resent that! I'm not his puppet. I have my own will. My own mind. I want to be with him. I want to see him. I miss him, even when it's only been hours."

Diana shook her head. "This isn't the way it should be. It's all wrong, sick."

"Sick? You want to talk about sick? Sick is that slime on your face."

Diana's face bloomed into a green-coated smile. She ran her fingers down her cheek, making three pink stripes then glanced at the smudge collected on her fingertips. With a wicked grin Jane knew meant trouble, she flicked her fingers, sending that nasty stuff into Jane's face.

Some dripped from Jane's eyelashes. She swiped at it, but it merely smeared into her eyes, which left her blinking to clear her hazy vision. "That was not nice, brat."

"Neither is you ducking out of our night out."

"I promise I'll make it next week."

Diana scowled. "Liar."

"Promise. Now, give me a tissue. I can't go see Josh looking like this."

"It's kiwi and oatmeal. It's good for your skin. In fact, you're showing a little age these days—"

"Just hand me the tissue!"

Diana thrust a box at Jane then slammed the door. Calling, "It had better be important or there will be hell to pay!"

"I'm sure it is."

After doing her best to wipe off the offensive facemask, Jane dashed to her car and drove to Josh's place, not surprised when he met her at the front door. His expression was forced, like he was trying hard to look happy. His smile was empty.

"Hi." She stepped into the foyer, her heart in her throat. "What's wrong?"

"I have to tell you something. Something important. But later. Can we have some dinner first?"

A million possibilities shot through her brain, but none of them made sense. "Okay."

It took every ounce of willpower she possessed not to ask him questions about whatever was weighing so heavily on his shoulders, but she resisted. She followed him into his gorgeous formal dining room and they sat at the end of a dining table long enough to comfortably seat at least thirty.

She'd never imagined herself living amid such extravagance, but she just might be—barring any unforeseen complications. She had the distinct impression tonight might just determine whether they would go further.

Her heart ached a tiny bit at the thought of spending even a single day without Josh.

"I'm sorry for ruining your plans tonight." He poked at his salad.

"To tell you the truth, I'm not disappointed at all. Diana wanted to hit that nightclub where you took me to dance. I'm not much for club hopping. It's just not my scene. And that one, well, no offense, but the crowd there was a little strange." She recalled the bizarre array of people she'd seen there, many of them pale-faced, wearing black. Now that she thought about it, there's been something distinctly unsettling about the way some of them had looked at her. Almost like she was…dessert.

He smiled, but the expression still lacked the usual Josh sparkle. "I'm so glad you came tonight."

She studied the tossed greens on her plate. There was something a little odd about them. She took a taste. Bitter. Yuck. Thankful she wasn't starving, since she'd swallowed a diet shake on the way to Diana's, she pushed the salad plate away. "Did you have a rough day?"

"No. Things are going well—at work, that is. But I'm feeling the call of home. I'm ready to slow down, start a family."

That didn't sound bad. Considering the palace he called home, she imagined he had enough money to retire comfortably. "I can appreciate that. Work isn't exactly my favorite thing these days, either."

"Quit."

"Music to my ears, but I have bills to pay."

"I'll pay them. Just give them to me."

She thought about it for a moment. Tempting, yes. Responsible, no. "I can't do that."

"Why not? In case you haven't noticed," he said, sweeping his arm and motioning around the room, "I have a bit of money."

"Believe me, I've noticed. I'd have to be blind not to notice. But those are my bills. I should pay them."

"Then work for me."

"No. I hate waitressing." Images of her last attempt at that career slashed through her mind. She had been absolutely inept. The worst.

"I would never hire you as a waitress."

What did that mean? What job would she be hired to do? "Really?"

"You're much too intelligent. More management material than waitress material."

"Well, I guess I should take that as a compliment, but I don't like the idea of being a manager, either. Restaurant managers work crappy hours, nights, weekends..."

"Being the owner's wife means you work choice hours."

She cringed inside but didn't show it. "That's not exactly the best way to make friends at work. No, thanks. I think I'm better off working somewhere else."

"Okay. Then let me ask you this, if you could work anywhere, do anything, what would you do?"

"I don't know." She'd never thought about it. At least, not since she'd graduated high school. Work was something she did to pay bills. It wasn't fulfilling. It wasn't fun—most days. There were exceptions, thanks to Diana. What if she could choose anything? What would she like?

"Think about it." He pushed away another empty plate, and Jane glanced down at her own, still full. He nodded toward her food. "Are you finished?"

"Yeah. I wasn't very hungry. Sorry."

"That's okay. Let's go talk." He took her hand and led her into a dark paneled library, a cozy room that smelled good—like libraries always did. She sat next to him on a leather sofa, ever conscious of how gorgeous he was, but more worried about what he was about to say. He scrubbed his hands through his hair, messing his flirty curls and sending them every which way. "I have no idea how to tell you this."

This was something big. She'd never seen him like this—his eyes avoiding her, his body restless, hands hopping from one inane task to another. Since she'd first stepped into the house, the only thing that had been normal was the man's huge appetite. "What is it?"

He stopped the useless motion and finally met her gaze. "This is going to be a big shock to you."

"Just tell me."

He visibly swallowed. "Before I tell you, I just want you to know I really do love you. Like I've never loved anyone. And I'll die if I lose you."

She smacked his knee. "Oh, for God's sake, just spit it out! The woman is supposed to be the dramatic one."

"I'm…a…shit!" He jumped up, and she followed him.

"No, you're not a shit, but you are pissing me off. Give it to me straight. Are you a drug lord? A mobster?"

He chuckled, but it sounded forced. "No. Nothing like that."

She wasn't relieved.

"I'm a selkie."

"A what?"

"You might say a merman."

She studied his face for a moment, waiting for his grim expression to break, for the teasing smile to burst through.

It didn't.

He couldn't be serious! She smiled, and he mirrored the expression, sort of. Good God, he was serious!

Oh… "A merman," she repeated.

"Yes."

"There aren't any such things."

"I know your kind believes that, but we are real."

"My kind?"

"Humans."

"And you're not my kind?"

"No, I'm a selkie."

If this wasn't so pathetic, it might be funny. She physically felt her heart explode into tiny razor sharp fragments.

She'd been right all along. He was too good to be true. Josh DeWet, the man of her dreams, the man she'd fallen in love with, was a nutcase. Damn! It wasn't fair. "Okay. So, you're not from Canada, then?"

"No. I mean, our family lives in the ocean. Once a year, we return to the land for a religious celebration, and then we return to the water."

She wasn't buying this, but what the hell could she say? Either he was looking for a creative way to dump her, or he truly believed what he was saying and needed some drugs, pronto. "And why would you lie to me?"

"At first, I wished to mate with you and then return home."

"Mate? Like produce offspring?"

"Precisely. We cannot mate with our own kind. Inbreeding weakens our bloodlines and causes disease."

Now this was getting scary! She immediately wondered if she might be pregnant. He'd intended on her getting pregnant. It was possible. Pregnant with a psycho's kid!

She wanted to cry.

He gripped her hand, and she pulled it away. "But you see, I couldn't do it. I couldn't leave you. I love you."

"This is all too much. You know, if you're looking for an out, an easy way to dump me, you can just tell me this isn't working. No need to make up stories." She forced a smile and waited for him to admit he wanted to end the relationship.

He shook his head. "No. I want you to marry me and come home with me."

"To Canada?"

"To the sea."

Now she knew his egg was cracked! "Okay. But how do I breathe?"

"That's a simple hurdle to overcome. You need a bone marrow transplant."

"What?" She jumped up. That was what cancer patients got. That procedure was dangerous. That procedure was painful, and ugly, and miserable. Why would she voluntarily go through with it when she wasn't sick? "I need to go home."

"I'll have the driver take you. You're too upset to drive."

"I'm fine. Really." She practically ran toward the door, not easy considering the room was tipping and swaying like a carnival funhouse.

Josh caught her shoulders and drilled his gaze into her eyes. "I'm not insane. I'm not lying. And I love you. Please believe me."

She forced another smile. No telling what he might do if he got mad. "I do believe you. I'm just not sure what to make of it."

"I'll call you tomorrow."

"That's fine." She broke free from his grasp and found her way to the front door, and without taking a final look back, walked out into the pitch black, started her car and drove home.

What an idiot she'd been! The signs had been there all along; she'd known he was too good to be true.

# Chapter Sixteen

*Accepting the most illogical possibility is sometimes the most logical thing to do.*

Diana shook her head and took a bite of her apple, the final course in a meal that was big enough to fill a football linebacker. "Oh Jane. I'm so sorry."

"Aren't you going to say 'I told you so'?" Jane stuffed her uneaten sandwich into her bag, spun around on the picnic table bench, resting against the table, and watched some children play with toy boats in a nearby pond. "You were right. I was jumping in way to fast. I didn't know him. I was so stupid!"

"You got swept up in it all. Hell! I can't blame you." Diana came around the table and sat next to Jane, hugging her shoulders. "He was good looking, rich, nice. Who would have thought he was a freak?"

"It has to be insanity, right? I mean, what else could it be?" She glanced at her watch, wishing the rest of the afternoon would simply fly by. Right now, more than anything she needed a nice, relaxing weekend. At home, alone.

"He could be a selkie for real," Diana teased, giving her shoulders an extra-hard squeeze.

"Yeah, sure. If selkies eat like pigs, have sexual appetites like rabbits, and conduct electricity like eels, maybe."

Diana dropped her hand. "Electricity?"

"Yeah. He did this weird thing with his hands. I saw electricity come from them. Why?"

"That's sort of weird. Don't you think?"

"I do, but I figured it was like some New Age healing thing, like that Reiki thing I read about."

With a shrug, Diana stood. "Must be." She gathered her trash and dropped it in a nearby can. "At least you didn't marry him. Wouldn't that be awful?"

"Yeah. He expected me to get a bone marrow transplant so I could live under the sea with him. Could you just imagine?"

They shared an empty laugh, and Jane felt her heart grow heavier. Had that been only last night? Already it felt like it had been weeks ago. It killed her being apart from him. How would she live a lifetime without him? How?

"It'll get easier. Promise," Diana said, basically reading her mind.

"How does someone I've known for such a short time become so damn important? How come with every heartbeat I'm away from him, I feel a little weaker? It's like he nourishes me."

"I know, sweetie."

"I don't know if you do. I've never felt anything like this. The whole world could go to hell. I just can't stand having things wrong between Josh and me. I'm going nuts without him."

"You'll be okay with time. It's just going to take a while. Your thing with Josh was short, but intense, and you got swept up in it. You have to give yourself some time to grieve."

She watched a little boy bend low and reach for his sailboat. He was so little, such a cutie. "I felt whole with Josh. Strong. Beautiful. Like I could conquer anything. I've lost that part of myself now. It was tied to him."

"No you haven't. It's still there."

The boy teetered on the concrete edge and then, arms flailing, legs kicking, in he went. "Oh my God!" She jumped to her feet.

Diana sprung up. "What?"

"That little boy!" Jane ran down the hill to the pond and dove into the water, swimming straight down to the child who was already limp at the bottom. Wrapping one arm around his chest, she pushed off the bottom and swam toward the surface. When she broke through, the sight of dozens of strangers standing nearby, calling to her, confused her for a moment, but she swam to the side and let the child's parent, or so she assumed, lift him from the water.

"Is he okay?" Diana asked Jane as she helped Jane climb over the concrete pond wall. "Look at you!" She dropped her gaze and Jane looked down.

She was a soaking wet mess. Clothes wet and tangled with weeds, hair streaming down her back, nylons torn, shoes lost. "I'm a mess."

"No, you're a hero!" Diana's expression was full of such pride, Jane felt herself glowing with embarrassment.

"No, I'm not. It was a little boy." She brushed past Diana to check and see how he was.

He lay in his father's arms, coughing like mad, but alive and breathing.

"I owe you his life," the father said. "Thank you. I went after his sister, and I saw Jimmy fall, but I couldn't get there... He could have..."

"I'm glad I could help. Is he okay?"

The man nodded, and a fireman approached from behind. Jane left, and only when she reached her car did she realize what she'd just done.

She dove into water to save a drowning child. She did that. Without fear. Without thinking. As if she'd been born swimming.

There was only one person to thank for that. One person who'd worked so hard to help her overcome her fear. One person who'd encouraged and supported her. Josh.

She had to thank him, if nothing more. He deserved no less.

When she sat in sat in her car, she called to Diana, "I'm going home for the rest of the day. I'll call you later."

"What are you up to?"

"I'll tell you later."

"You're going to talk to him, aren't you?"

"If he hadn't helped me, if he hadn't forced me to overcome my fear, I would never have gone after that little boy. I want to thank him. Tell him what he's done."

Since Diana could go back to work in a cab, Jane drove straight home to change her clothes.

After hopping on the net to read up on selkie lore and schizophrenia, she drove to his home. It was still early, mid-afternoon, and he wasn't home, but the butler welcomed her into the mansion and gave her free reign of the whole house. Jane took advantage of it, exploring every room she stumbled upon.

No doubt about it, Josh took that selkie thing seriously. Every space was decorated in a sea life theme. Various shades of blue colored every wall, and nearly every room had an aquarium in it. In the kitchen, the refrigerator and freezer were both stocked to the gills with seafood, fish, shrimp, crab.

Such a sad thing. How had he become so obsessed?

When hours passed, and she'd grown tired of wandering the huge building, she found her way to his bedroom and relaxed, slipping into a dream-filled sleep where he was swimming around her, and they were both surrounded by cool blue waters.

She felt his touch. Could he be real? Or was she still dreaming? She opened her eyes.

He smiled, his eyes glittering with mischief and happiness. "Hi."

Her heart nearly exploded with joy at seeing him, those eyes. His lips. The mole under his eye. "Hi." She blinked the sleep from her eyes and sat up. "Something happened today, and I needed to tell you."

He sat next to her. "What happened?"

"There was a little boy. He fell into the pond at the park, and I dove in and saved him. It was because of you. I would never have done that if it hadn't been for you."

"That's wonderful, but it was you. You did it. Your strength allowed it."

"Speaking of strength, or lack thereof, I'm sorry for running out like I did last night."

"You still don't believe me."

"No."

"Will you let me prove it to you?"

How would he do that?

Did she really want to know the truth? What if he was a selkie? "Okay."

He took her hands in his and pulled her from the bed. "We have to go somewhere."

A brief flash of unease coursed through her body but was quickly replaced by calm. "Okay." She followed him through the house and outside. The limo came to a stop to pick them up, without being summoned, and they rode the short distance to the beach they'd visited together on that wonderful day.

But this time it was dark, the sky a deep blue-black. Stars twinkled. The moon cast a silvery glow over the water's rippling surface.

Once out of the car, Josh led her to the water's edge. "I must come here every Friday at exactly midnight, and I must remain in the water until midnight Saturday. That's why you've never seen me on a Saturday afternoon."

Immediately, memories from that first night, his unusual pallor, surfaced. That had been Friday night. Midnight. A chill shot up Jane's spine and she shivered.

Could he be telling the truth? "What happens if you don't go to the water?" she asked.

"I die. The poisons in the air are too toxic for my body. And I must replenish the water that escapes into the air as well."

"Like a frog?"

He smiled, and she couldn't help appreciating the beauty of it, even in the dark. "In a way."

She glanced at her watch, surprised by the time. She'd slept for hours back at the house, and it was now near midnight.

What would she see in a few short minutes? She wasn't sure she could deal with it, whether she saw him change into a fish-man or not.

Josh shed his shirt, shoes, socks and pants, and she watched, enthralled by his sleek, muscled, body. He moved with such grace, even as he did the most mundane of tasks. As each heartbeat sounded in her ear, she waited for something, anything, to prove what he was.

Which did she hope for? Which was worse? For him to be some kind of mythological creature? Or for him to be delusional?

He motioned for her to join him as he sat on the sand, so near the lapping tide as the cool water slipped up over her feet, but she wrapped her arms around herself against the chill and sat next to him.

"No human is permitted to see the Transformation. It is written; it is our curse. After today, I will not be able to return to the surface, to you."

"You won't?"

He shook his head. "I love you. If you must see this to believe me, then so be it. But understand that I cannot return. Ever."

"So, how do I find you?"

"You must either go with me, now, or forget about me forever."

What kind of choice was that? "But you said I needed a bone marrow transplant to live underwater. How will I go with you?"

"I can breathe for you until we get to my world. It is in a protective dome. Our doctors can perform the transplant. Then you will be like us, like other marine mammals. We have a protein that allows us to carry extra oxygen in our bloodstream. We can hold our breath for hours. Or to be sure of this, we can wait up to a year to do the procedure."

Protein in the blood? Was it true? She knew whales and other animals did hold their breath, but she'd never read how.

It was possible.

She wasn't buying this…was she?

Was his skin turning gray? Maybe it was the cold. Or the strange color of the moonlight. A funny slapping sound hit the beach at her feet and she looked down.

Oh God!

She felt the world spinning. She hadn't just seen what she thought she'd seen. No way! His legs were not fusing into one, his feet twisting to the sides and bending into a fin.

She clamped her eyelids closed, swallowed several times, and waited for the dizziness to ease.

"I have to go now," he said. "You must make a choice. And once that choice is made, you cannot go back."

She opened her eyes and drew in a deep breath. He looked unreal, like a picture in fantasy art. His body was even bulkier than before, if that was possible, but where his skin had been sun-bronzed, now it was silver, a strange contrast to his gold hair. His legs were gone, replaced with one long tail covered with silver-blue scales. "Oh my God!"

"Do you love me?"

She did. She knew she did. But live under the sea? Where all her worst nightmares lurked?

"Do you trust me?"

He had always said if she was with him, nothing would happen to her. She looked into his eyes, and heard his voice inside her head. It vibrated through every part of her.

*You are carrying my child,* he said. *It is not my wish that you will raise him alone. Come. Be my wife. Our queen. I love you.*

She dropped her hand to her belly. "A child?"

He nodded. "My son. Our future king."

This was too much! She gripped her head in her hands, muffling the soft sound of the water splashing against the sandy shore. What should she do?

It was real!

She thought about Diana and Carmen. How they'd miss her. She hadn't even said goodbye. Her job—okay, she wouldn't miss that.

But what about the warmth of the sun on a summer day? She'd miss that. And the smell of flowers and freshly mown grass. She'd miss those.

There was one thing—one person—she'd miss more than anything. There was one man she could no more live without than air, and he was being carried away on the tide.

"Wait!" She dashed into the sea, the water pulling at her shins. "Don't go!"

He turned to face her, his head bobbing above the surface. "Come to me. You must come on your own."

She ran, pushing through the heavy water, eager to break the distance between them, but it was as if the water wouldn't let her. It rolled, forming high walls, obscuring him from her view, and no matter how hard she fought, she found herself being swept back toward shore.

Exhausted, and unable to see him over the bulging tide, she sat on the sand and did the only thing she could do. She cried, hollered out in frustration, then cursed the sea for being so damn big and strong.

# Chapter Seventeen

*Doubt paralyses the strongest of men.*

He was gone.

Damn it! She hadn't really been convinced she wanted to go, even as she'd thrashed and kicked through the water.

Until now. Now, she felt empty and alone. He was gone, and he could never come back.

What had she done? She'd hesitated too long, and look what it had cost her. How would she live without him? And what if he said was true? What if she was carrying his baby? She shouted a few more choice words.

This wasn't the way it was supposed to be; this isn't what she wanted.

"I love you, Josh!" she yelled into the splashing, crashing surf. "I will always love you." Then she stood and pushing against the tide that had seemed to have changed directions, she started moving toward the open water.

But now, instead of being swept inland, she seemed to be pushed out to sea, no matter how hard she fought it. It was as if the water had a will.

She fought it, panicking, fearful she'd drown without Josh. Still, it pulled her deeper and deeper out to sea, until she was floating, the land beyond her reach, the shore too distant to see over the waves.

Oh God! She would die out here! "Josh!"

Something gripped her waist and pulled her under, and she fought for a moment, thrashing her hands to bring her back to the surface. Then, she saw his face and she relaxed.

*I'm here,* he said in her head.

*I thought you were gone. You said you couldn't come back. You said I had to come to you.*

*I had to wait. You had to choose. You had to truly wish to be with me, or the tide would not turn. It followed your lead, carrying you to me.*

*It followed my lead? Not in my book. If it had, I'd have been out here a lot sooner.*

*It's just like humans to fight against the tide they themselves command, but once they learn to follow its will, they're rewarded. I'm glad you chose me.*

*Me, too.*

*Let's begin our journey.* He kissed her, filling her lungs with sweet, pure air. He shed her clothes, his fingertips tracing the curves of her body, and heating her against the chill of the sea. She pressed her body to his, eager to feel his strength. Eager to meld her body to his, her legs wrapped around his waist, and his thick erection prodded her pussy.

His growl rumbled through her body, electrifying nerve endings everywhere. Foreign sounds echoed in her ears, and new tastes seeped into her mouth. The silky water caressed her skin, soaking up the heat bursting from her core as her need for Josh's touch grew.

He slipped two fingers inside, stroking in and out.

She bit back a cry of agony and leaned back, weightless and floating. He held her hips with one hand, his other carrying her away on a tide of bliss as he circled over her clit before plunging deep inside again. Then his tongue took the place of his fingers, lapping her folds and teasing her clit.

She was drifting, falling, careening to a far off land, yet all she cared about was the feel of his touch, the taste of the air he blew into her mouth, and the sound of his voice in her head.

Her eyelids fell closed, and when they opened, there were more silver faces surrounding her. People she'd never seen. Men and women.

*She is my queen,* Josh said. *I have chosen.*

*She is a human,* a woman with flowing blonde hair said.

*She will bear me many children. She is strong and able. She will make a great queen. You must welcome her as our tradition dictates.*

Her pussy aching with need, her body aflame, her legs still wide apart, her hips still gripped firmly in Josh's hand, she waited. What was their tradition? Couldn't the creatures wait? Wasn't it obvious they were busy at the moment? *Um, Josh? Can't this tradition thing wait a little while? I mean, I was so close…*

She tried to pull her legs closed. There was something very uncomfortable about being open and exposed like that, before all those strange beings.

*No. Remain as you are. This is our tradition, and your deepest fantasy.* He laid her upon a flat rock balanced atop a taller rock that resembled a pillar and then he breathed into her mouth.

*My deepest fantasy? I don't think so.* She closed her mouth, trapping the air inside, and shut her eyes against the faces hovering around her. Ghostlike, their eyes big, they studied her as if she were a specimen.

Yet, she had to admit, her pussy was throbbing. There was something very erotic about the experience.

*He is my son and future king. As his wife, your responsibilities will be many. We welcome you, and bless your body so that it will be fruitful and will bring many babies.* The woman ran her hands down Jane's body, from the tips of her collarbone to her toes.

Another voice said, *He is my brother, and keeper of all things dear to our people. We worship your body as the vessel of his seed, wishing you many fruitful years and blessings.* Another round of touches traveled up and down her body. Light and fleeting, they tickled her, leaving a trail of goosebumps in their wake.

*He is my son,* a male voice said. The voice was deep and commanding, much like Josh's. *And my future heir. He holds the future of our people in his hands. As his wife, you must protect that future, bear it with pride, nourish and nurture it until it is brought to maturity. We worship your body as the giver of life, the chosen one to nurture the future of our people.* His touch was more firm as it traveled down over her breasts and stomach and then down her legs.

*Now, we must bless your fertility,* he commanded.

*What does that mean? Please tell me these people aren't into group sex. That's never been my thing.*

*Have no fear,* Josh said in her head. *Give in to the pleasure. They are preparing you for me. Let them.*

*Preparing how?* Jane opened her eyes and met Josh's reassuring gaze, and then she nodded. Two women reached for her legs, wrapping their hands around her knees and lifting them, forcing her legs far apart.

*Oh God!* Jane released a blast of air, and Josh covered her mouth with his, filling her lungs again. His tongue dipped into her mouth, stroking hers, and sending hot sparks between her legs.

*They are preparing you for me,* he repeated before drawing away. *Close your eyes.*

*Okay, I can handle this. It's a tradition. I'm sure it's nothing kinky…not too kinky, I hope.* She did as he told her to, but opened them with the first touch. A woman was running a handful of green stuff up and down her body, chanting in some language she couldn't understand. Another approached with bright flowers of some kind.

Flowers? In the sea?

The woman set them upon her stomach, low, over her womb. Only then did she realize they weren't flowers. They were hard. Carved out of something, crystal? Beautiful.

More voices joined the chanting, and hands reached from all directions toward her, resting on every part of her body, her tits, stomach, pussy, legs, ass. Currents of electricity shot from them, zapped up and down her spine and exploded in her womb, feeling like a million tongues teasing her clit.

Her stomach muscles clenched into a tight ball, lifting her hips higher, and her thigh muscles pulled, spreading her legs further.

*That's it, love,* Josh said in a honey-smooth voice. *Give in to the pleasure. Let them worship your body and bless our love.*

The chanting picked up in pace, and with it, the teasing strokes over her clit. Between the strange sounds in her head and the agonizingly erotic touches on her pussy and ass, she thought she'd go mad with need. Her body was flaming hot, her blood like lava, carrying that heat upwards and out. A pool of it collected in her gut.

She needed him. Inside.

*Josh! Fuck me.*

Her pussy clamped closed around its own emptiness, eager to be filled. She felt her ass cheeks being spread. The chanting changed, becoming as urgent as the need building inside her.

*Patience, Love. They're not through with the blessing yet. Show me how much my love pleases you.* He breathed for her again, filling her lungs. He tasted sweet and musty. Of her juices. *I drink from you.* He drifted to the end of the rock and joined the chanting. As she looked down, she saw him drop his head between her legs, and his tongue drew slow, lazy circles around her slit.

The women pulled at her legs, stretching her inner thigh muscles, but she gloried in the feeling, wanting to be open to him. It felt so right, surrendering her body to him like this, open, raw, nothing hidden.

*We will see our blessings received, the* man said. *Show us how you receive our blessings.*

*Come for them,* Josh whispered into her soul. *Come for all of them, and welcome their blessings into your spirit.*

His words alone nearly sent her over the edge. With the help of one tight circle over her clit, she came, every muscle in her body pulsing in orgasm.

The people cheered and sang, and Josh kissed her. *You are now my wife and their queen. Welcome to your new kingdom.*

As the final twitches of her climax settled, she opened her eyes and saw what she hadn't seen before, a city of crystal, sparkling as the light of the distant sun shot through the deep waters and struck the cut facets.

*Come and see your new home.* Josh breathed into her mouth, took her hand, and she followed him into the glittering new world before her.

She glanced back and met the welcoming gazes of the people, the warm smiles and reverent bows.

*Our queen.*

She was a queen? Plain Jane. The woman who'd let fear run her life for years?

How could it be so? Yet, as she stood at the bottom of the sea, she stared at the city of crystal that was as real as anything she'd ever seen before.

Somehow, this was her new life. A life full of wonder and beauty, with the man she loved. That alone was enough for her.

She was in heaven.

# Chapter Eighteen

*Irony makes life interesting.*

"You look like death warmed over," Diana proclaimed the minute she stepped into Jane's hospital room, surgical mask in one hand, latex gloves in the other. "In fact, I came here ready to throttle you. You'd better be damn grateful you're so sick." She hooked the mask over her face, slipped on the gloves and shook her head. "Look at you!"

*Diana, it's good to see you too. Glad to hear you haven't worried about me too bad the past twelve months.* Jane forced a smile. "Thank you for pointing out the bright side to getting a bone marrow transplant. Stupid me, I thought it was plain misery."

"So, when are you going to tell me what happened to you? One minute we were getting ready for a girls' night out and the next, you're gone. And nothing, no calls, no letters. For twelve months!"

"Sorry."

She plopped onto the mattress, resting her rear end next to Jane's knees. "The least you could have done was call me, you little bitch! I hate you for making me worry for a whole year!"

"I didn't have access to a phone."

"Bullshit! You could have found a phone. I won't hear any excuses."

"Fine. I should have found a phone." *Why did I call her? I feel like death. I don't need a lecture.* Jane let her eyelids fall closed and wished she could undo what she'd done by calling Diana several days ago. She glanced at the clock. Good God, it had only been three minutes since Diana had arrived! How long were visiting hours?

"The police will be happy to hear they can close the missing person's case."

"See? A bright side. Now, will you quit punishing me? I just had a bone marrow transplant, for God's sake. I'm miserable enough."

Diana sighed. "I suppose I could lighten up a bit. So, I'm assuming you married Josh?"

"Yes."

She clucked her tongue and pulling the mask down, scowled like only Diana could do. "You didn't even invite me to your wedding!"

"It was a spur of the moment decision."

"No excuse. You know I would have died before I'd miss your wedding."

*You would have died if you'd tried to attend.* "I'm sorry. Will you please forgive me? It was selfish for me to run off and get married the way I did."

"That's better." Diana's gaze visibly traveled over Jane's face. "And now you're sick? Is it cancer?"

"No."

"No? Well what other reason would you have to get a bone marrow transplant?"

"It's hard to explain. It's a medical condition. My blood doesn't have a protein it needs—"

Diana waved her hand, cutting off Jane's explanation, not that she cared. The less she tried to explain the better.

"I've never understood medical jargon," Diana said, toying with Jane's IV line. "I'll take your word for it. So, when will you be out of here? And why did you come all the way up here to a Canadian hospital?"

"This hospital has a doctor who specializes in my condition. And he says I'll be able to leave as soon as my blood count rises to a safe level, maybe a week or two."

"That's great! Will you be coming home?"

"Not the home you're thinking of."

"Will you at least give me your phone number and address so I can stay in touch with you?"

"I can't."

Diana crossed her arms over her chest. "Why the hell not?"

"I don't have one."

"Everyone has an address, even the Eskimos living on the North Pole. Why did you call and make me drive all the way up here if you don't want to be friends any longer? What the hell is going on?"

"Diana, I don't know how to explain."

"Well, you'd better start trying something, because I'm going to cry if you don't."

*Oh God. Not that*! "Okay. Um… "*Shit! She's going to think I need more than a bone marrow transplant if I tell her the truth.* "Josh belongs to a very unique breed—"

"Breed? As in dog?"

"No." *And I thought this was going to be hard? It's going to be impossible!* "That was the wrong expression. Unique community of people. They live in a very remote place, without electricity and phones and microwave ovens..."

"Like the Amish?"

"Not really."

"It sounds like hell."

Jane felt a smile pulling at her lips. "Actually, it's wonderful, but I don't expect you to think so."

"No electricity? Well, all I can say is don't expect me to visit very often."

"Fair enough." Jane drew in her first deep breath in ages. Had she succeeded in easing Diana's curiosity? "So, you know I'm okay. I'm alive and kicking, and we can meet once a year here in Canada if you like."

"This town isn't so bad. It's kind of pretty, actually."

"You can tell me what's going on in your life. Anything to report?"

"Not like what you have. I met a nice guy at that bar we tried to get into. Remember that place? We finally got in there. He owns the place. His name is Max."

"Max?" She knew that name! *Oh, boy, are you in for the ride of your life! Hold on, baby!* "That sounds like a very nice name. Tell me more. Is it serious?"

"No. Not yet, but he sure knows how to fuck. And he eats like there's no tomorrow. Oh, and he does this crazy, kinky thing with electricity... Hey, didn't you tell me that Josh did that too?"

"I may have." Jane felt herself growing sleepy. "I'm sure you'll be very happy together."

"I hope you're right. He's filthy rich. You should see his house!" Diana dropped her feet to the floor and headed toward the door. "Well, see you next year. I'm glad you called."

"Yes. Me too. I'll see you next year. If not sooner," Jane said with a smile. *I can just imagine your reaction when Max transforms in front of you.*

No sooner was Diana gone, than Jane drifted off into a deep, healing sleep.

Her condition continued to improve every day, with only a few minor setbacks, and she was released exactly one week later, the day of the Festival of the Moon.

At eleven on the dot, Josh arrived at the hospital, with their beautiful three-month son in tow, a bright smile on his handsome face, and a bouquet of flowers in his fist. "How are you feeling?" He looked worried, his brows hovering a little lower than normal.

"I'm ready to get out of here." As hospital procedure dictated, she waited for a volunteer to arrive with a wheelchair, and rode the short distance to the exit in peace, thankful to have her husband at her side, and her baby on her lap.

Two whole weeks of being away from them had been murder. She nuzzled her son, inhaling his sweet breath and staring at his tiny features. They were identical to his father's. The perfect miniature. She wouldn't have wanted it any other way. She kissed the wispy white hair on the top of his head.

She settled herself in the car as Josh secured the baby in his car seat and then took his own. Admiring his gorgeous profile as he turned the key and glanced around the car, she gripped Josh's hand and squeezed. "I did it. Will it really work?"

"Yes. You'll see. Now, you'll be comfortable, able to hold your breath just like we do."

"That's amazing."

"Amazing? No, you're amazing." He leaned over and kissed her gently before shifting into drive and pulling away from the hospital. That brief kiss didn't even begin to be long enough, though, and she bit back a frustrated sigh.

"After tonight, we will be free to truly begin our new lives," he continued.

"I hope we'll have some quiet time to get…reacquainted," she teased. "It's been two weeks, and I've missed you."

He glanced at her as he pulled the car up to a red traffic light. "I've missed you, too. It was nearly impossible for me to stay away all this time. But don't worry. I have special plans for you tonight, right after the festival."

"I can't wait. Want to give me a sneak peek?" She tipped her head and tried for a come-hither look.

He chuckled—so much for the effect she was shooting for—shook his head, and set the car into motion again. "No time for that. We must attend the festival. It's tradition. But once it's over, at exactly midnight, you're mine."

"I hope the baby will sleep—"

"My mother's on baby duty. I already cleared it with her."

"That's very generous."

"It's purely selfish on her part. She wants a granddaughter."

A lump formed in Jane's throat, and she hacked. "Already? Josh Junior is only three months old, and I'm still recovering from the transplant."

"She doesn't understand. Remember, she did it, and if it didn't kill her, she figures it's good for everyone."

"That woman is tough as nails."

"And as good as gold. Someday I'll have to tell you my folk's story. It's really something."

"I'm looking forward to it." She watched the pretty northern Canadian scenery as they drove the short distance to the cottage, happy for the momentary peace and quiet. She knew that would change before long.

It took less time than she thought. Joshua Junior began wailing before they reached their destination, and she was forced to sing every lullaby she knew to keep him quiet. Luckily, their drive was short. No one should be forced to listen to her singing for more than a few short minutes, it was absolutely horrible, faintly resembling the squawk of a dying crow.

When they arrived at the cottage, Jane tended to the source of Josh Junior's discomforts while his father prepared for the festival. He had to wear an ornate costume adorned with a shimmery substance that looked like flattened pearls. Having been on land for several weeks, his skin had tanned, a nice contrast to the costume. He was not just a handsome man. He was a beautiful man.

The reigning king, now that his father had abdicated the throne.

Her husband.

In many ways, it still seemed a dream.

After he prepared, he helped Jane dress in her costume, a clingy, sexy number that hugged her breasts and hips. The bodice was open in the center, the neckline diving between her breasts and landing just above her belly button. The skirt was long in the back, micro-mini in the front—not the best design considering she just had a baby and the stretch marks on her thighs and hips were still candy-apple red.

Even so, she felt beautiful. And sexy…and like it might fall off at the slightest breeze.

They dressed Josh Junior in his snappiest outfit, and headed to the beach, not surprised to see everyone was already there.

A giant tent stood just shy of the water, and inside were rows and rows of tables, food heaped on giant plates. At the front, closest to the water, stood an altar-looking thing. Higher than a table, it was covered in white tablecloths and had some sort of symbol sewn into the front.

The most stunning woman Jane had ever seen stood behind it. She practically radiated light.

"Who is that?"

"Our goddess, Coventina. Tonight is a festival to honor her, and thank her for her continued blessings." He pulled Jane's hand, leading her to the altar.

Jane reluctantly followed, silently rehearsing a suitable greeting. What did one say to a goddess? "Hey, how's it been in god-land?"

Josh cradled Junior in his arms and knelt before the shimmering woman. She said a blessing in some bizarre screeching voice that reminded Jane of seagulls. With a tip of his head, he encouraged Jane to do the same. As they left the goddess, he whispered, "You don't know how blessed you've just become."

She watched the stream of fellow selkies making their way to the altar behind them. "I'll take your word for it. Now what?"

"We eat!" He led her to a table, helped her settle and leaving Junior with her, he left to fill two plates with food. Returning, he set a plate before her and then took his seat.

More seafood! Good thing she'd learned to tolerate it, or she'd be starved to death by now.

As had become common, her appetite was huge, and she ate a ton, although it wasn't easy. Between watching Josh do obscene—but very provocative—things with his tongue while he ate, and juggling Junior, she couldn't exactly concentrate on what she was doing. The man made a sexy promise with every slurp, lick and bite of his food. Who knew crab and squid could be so erotic! Worse, he had a restless hand that tended to want to wander between her legs every few minutes. By the time they were through eating, her body was the constitution of a jellyfish.

"One more thing." Josh grinned and pulled her outside of the tent. "When the moon is at its fullest, we must..."

"Fuck each other's brains out?" she suggested.

"No." He gave her that grin that left her staggering and giddy. "Although you'd have no complaints from me."

"Then, what do we have to do?"

"Form a series of concentric circles, kneel and say a prayer."

"Oh. Okay." Did she feel stupid! "Well, you can't blame me for thinking the other, after our orgasmic wedding ceremony."

"Believe me, I like the way you think." He ran his hand down her back and squeezed her ass cheek. "As soon as we're through with the prayer, you're mine."

As Josh said, just before midnight, they formed a series of circles within circles with the other selkies—there were a lot of them, hundreds. Then they kneeled in the sand and said a prayer, again in that bizarre language that was only theirs. Finally, they left Junior with Josh's smiling mother and half-walked, half-ran to the cottage. Jane felt giddy and silly, like a naughty schoolgirl about to make out with her boyfriend behind the football bleachers. She tugged on her flimsy dress as she ran, enjoying the feeling of the cool, salty air on her skin.

Jane was completely undressed before she reached the cabin's door, and Josh was undressed soon after. Feeling a little brazen, and wanting to punish Josh a little for all the teasing he did during the festival, she tried a little wrestling maneuver she'd learned in self-defense class, knocking him to the floor. Feeling a little powerful after that bit of success, she leaned over him and took his cock into her mouth, not even bothering with the little stuff. Instead, she opened her mouth wide and swallowed him to the base, teasing his balls and ass with her hands.

He growled and, gripping her hair in his hands, pulled her head away. "You! That's...oh! That's not fair."

"What, dear? Don't you like?" Giving him an intentionally wicked grin, she fisted as much of his erection as she could and pumped up and down.

"It's been much too long."

"For you and me both."

He scowled and then in a ninja-like maneuver, turned the tables, gently flipping her over and leaving her flat on her back under him.

Not deterred, she lifted her legs and wrapped them around his waist, grinding her pussy into him. "Do you want me, lover?"

"You know I do." He pinned her shoulders to the floor with his hands and kissed her. His tongue and lips worked magic, lighting mini-fires all over her body. His hands dropped to her breasts, pinching her nipples and kneading their fullness.

She moaned, lost and dizzy from need.

He broke the kiss, and she lunged forward, trying to capture his mouth again.

"Now, this is better. I like to be in control. I'm the king. You must never forget that."

As he tip-toed his fingertips down her stomach, she held her breath. Those same fingers pulled at her labia, and she drew her legs back and apart, welcoming his touch and eager to be filled. A thick finger pushed into her pussy, and she sighed.

"I am your king," he murmured.

"Yes…"

"You serve me." He pushed a second finger inside, and she groaned. "For always." He gently pressed a third finger into her ass, and she gritted her teeth and cried out.

"Yes! Yes!"

"Do you want me?" he whispered into her ear.

"Oh, yes!" She writhed on the slick floor, her spine grinding into the pine. The smell of sea and salt and man filled her nose and lungs. The taste of him lingered on her tongue. The vision of him nude, his face tense with urgent, raw, hunger, played through her mind.

He swept her into his arms, taking her completely by surprise, and carried her into the bedroom. Glazed-eyed, she blinked as she clung to his wide shoulders and enjoyed the way his chorded muscles worked under his silky skin.

He was the strongest, sexiest man she'd ever met. And he was hers. For always.

"Yes, love. I am yours. Forever. I could never love another. You have my heart and my soul." He set her on the bed. "And now, I'll show you how much I love you." He pulled her legs apart and standing on the floor, he bent over to taste her.

As his tongue slipped between her labia, and his fingers slipped into her pussy, she arched her back, pressing her head into the bed.

"I love you more than life itself, and I will spend the rest of my life showing you how happy I am to have you as my wife."

As he thrust his cock deep inside, she soared toward orgasm with his sweet words echoing in her head.

This was the most precious gift of all: Josh's never-ending love.

She might only see the stars and the sky once a year. She might only see her dearest friends for a few hours each year. She might spend her life in the deep, blue ocean where her worst nightmares used to lurk.

Even a minute without Josh was a lifetime of hell, and now, thanks to a miracle, she would never have to endure hell again.

*The End*

*Enjoy this excerpt from*

PRIVATE GAMES

*Sure, that's all Detroit needs: three lunatic women running around in clothing that could barely be legal and putting themselves in asinine situations…so why am I even considering playing along?*

Maddy Beaudet gave her two closest friends, Candace and Nic, an intimidating stare, or so she hoped. But the resulting laughter peeling through her living room suggested she'd failed. Miserably. Not that she was surprised. Her visage was never one most people would call intimidating.

"Oh, come on, party-pooper." Candace drained her glass and set it on the coffee table before reaching for the wine bottle. "You said it yourself. You need a change."

Maddy snatched the bottle away before her well-meaning but half-cocked friend refilled her glass again. In the process, she knocked her cat from his favorite spot, curled up on her lap. She reached for him, but he snubbed her. "Sorry, Jack, but one more dose and that woman would be near impossible to reason with." Knowing it took him an hour, maybe two, to quit sulking—the animal was no better than a man—she turned to her friends. "Yeah, a change. As in a new job. Maybe some new clothes. Nothing major…like this!"

"It isn't major. It's a simple game among friends, for crying out loud. Now, give me that bottle."

"No way. And the game you're suggesting isn't just your run of the mill game. It's a man-chasing contest." She lifted her hand, holding the bottle out of Candace's reach. "That's…that's…"

"A hell of a lot of fun! Is there any other kind of game?" Nic said behind her, right before she filched the bottle from Maddy and handed it to Candace.

"Word games. Board games. Football games." Maddy groaned as she watched Candace grin and drain the remaining wine from the bottle. "You have no idea what you're doing."

Nic nodded. "Oh, yes I do."

"What women, graduated from elementary school, participate in such ridiculous contests?"

"Lots of them. It's the latest craze. It was even on *Oprah.* I got this on the Internet. It's the number one seller on all the major online retailers." Candace stood up and shook and gyrated like she did on a nightclub dance floor. Her gold hair whipped around like an enraged mop, if there was such a thing. "Relax, you need to shake things up a bit."

"Yeah, shake things up," Nic echoed.

Maddy swallowed a chuckle at Candace and poked her index finger at Nic. "I don't need any more help from you."

"Oh, yes you do."

She scowled at her traitorous friend before turning back to the hyperactive woman in front of her.

Candace looked like she was preparing to run a marathon. Hopping up and down, she half-sung, "You have no idea what might happen."

"If I jump up and down like that, I might bust loose from this bra."

"We better put this away for safe keeping until we get back." Candace gathered the game board and pieces, tossed them in the box and then shoved the deck of Challenge cards in her purse. Then she reached down and gripped Maddy's hands. "Worse things could happen. By the way, that bra does nothing for you."

"Yeah. Like I could lose my two thousand bucks."

"We all put in the same money. That was the deal. Just think about it. You could win! The trip of a lifetime. You've got a thirty-percent chance." With a yank Candace pulled Maddy to her feet and headed toward the door. "Let's go."

"Go where?"

"Shopping first. And then you pull your first Challenge card, and we're going along to make sure you go through with it."

Maddy dragged her feet as she half-walked, half-slunk onto the porch. "How thoughtful."

"It's my pleasure." Candace slammed the door behind them as they headed out to her car and then pushed Maddy toward the passenger side. "Someday you'll thank me."

"I doubt that."

# About the author:

After penning numerous romances bordering on sweet, Tawny Taylor realized her tastes ran toward the steamier side of romance, and she wrote her first erotic romance, Tempting Fate. Her second book, also a contemporary, Wet and Wilde, spotlights a water-phobic divorcee and a sexy selkie whom no woman could resist.

Tawny has been told she's sassy, brazen, and knows what she likes. So, it comes as no surprise that the heroines in her novels would be just those kinds of women. And her heroes...well, they are inspired by the most unlikely men. Mischievous, playful, they know exactly how to push those fiery heroines' buttons.

Combining two strong-willed characters takes a certain finesse, something Tawny learned while studying psychology in college. And writing pages of dialogue dripping with sensual undertones and innuendo has also been a learned task, one Tawny has undertaken with gusto.

It is Tawny's fondest wish her readers enjoy each and every spicy, sex-peppered page!

Tawny welcomes mail from readers. You can write to her c/o Ellora's Cave Publishing at 1337 Commerce Drive, Suite 13, Stow OH 44224.

## Why an electronic book?

We live in the Information Age—an exciting time in the history of human civilization in which technology rules supreme and continues to progress in leaps and bounds every minute of every hour of every day. For a multitude of reasons, more and more avid literary fans are opting to purchase e-books instead of paperbacks. The question to those not yet initiated to the world of electronic reading is simply: *why?*

1. *Price.* An electronic title at Ellora's Cave Publishing runs anywhere from 40-75% less than the cover price of the exact same title in paperback format. Why? Cold mathematics. It is less expensive to publish an e-book than it is to publish a paperback, so the savings are passed along to the consumer.
2. *Space.* Running out of room to house your paperback books? That is one worry you will never have with electronic novels. For a low one-time cost, you can purchase a handheld computer designed specifically for e-reading purposes. Many e-readers are larger than the average handheld, giving you plenty of screen room. Better yet, hundreds of titles can be stored within your new library—a single microchip. (Please note that Ellora's Cave does not endorse any specific brands. You can check our website at www.ellorascave.com for customer recommendations we make available to new consumers.)

3. *Mobility*. Because your new library now consists of only a microchip, your entire cache of books can be taken with you wherever you go.
4. *Personal preferences are accounted for*. Are the words you are currently reading too small? Too large? Too...**ANNOYING**? Paperback books cannot be modified according to personal preferences, but e-books can.
5. *Innovation*. The way you read a book is not the only advancement the Information Age has gifted the literary community with. There is also the factor of what you can read. Ellora's Cave Publishing will be introducing a new line of interactive titles that are available in e-book format only.
6. *Instant gratification*. Is it the middle of the night and all the bookstores are closed? Are you tired of waiting days—sometimes weeks—for online and offline bookstores to ship the novels you bought? Ellora's Cave Publishing sells instantaneous downloads 24 hours a day, 7 days a week, 365 days a year. Our e-book delivery system is 100% automated, meaning your order is filled as soon as you pay for it.

Those are a few of the top reasons why electronic novels are displacing paperbacks for many an avid reader. As always, Ellora's Cave Publishing welcomes your questions and comments. We invite you to email us at service@ellorascave.com or write to us directly at: 1337 Commerce Drive, Suite 13, Stow OH 44224.

Discover for yourself why readers can't get enough of the multiple award-winning publisher Ellora's Cave. Whether you prefer e-books or paperbacks, be sure to visit EC on the web at www.ellorascave.com for an erotic reading experience that will leave you breathless.